A Crabby Book

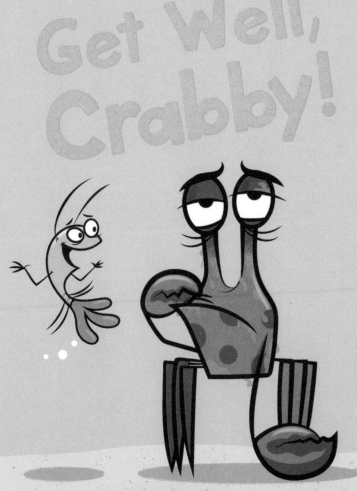

Get Well, Crabby!

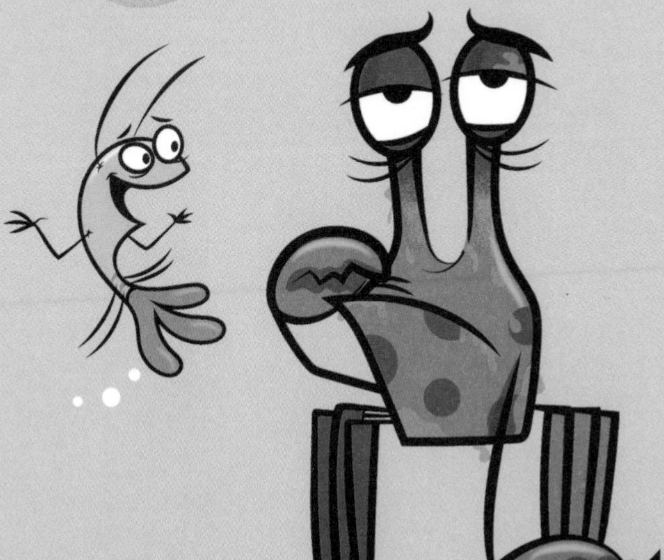

ACORN™
SCHOLASTIC INC.

Jonathan Fenske

To Jen and Eric, doctors of medicine **and** friendship!

Library of Congress Cataloging-in-Publication Data

Names: Fenske, Jonathan, author, illustrator.

Title: Get well, Crabby! / Jonathan Fenske.

Description: First edition. | New York : Acorn/Scholastic Inc, 2022. |

Series: A Crabby book ; 4

Summary: When Crabby gets sick, Plankton is determined to play doctor and take care of his friend, even if Crabby does not want the help—until Crabby realizes that he can get Plankton to do all of his household chores.

Identifiers: LCCN 2021022307 | ISBN 9781338767827 (paperback) | ISBN 9781338767834 (hardback)

Subjects: LCSH: Crabs—Juvenile fiction. | Plankton—Juvenile fiction. | Friendship—Juvenile fiction. | Conduct of life—Juvenile fiction. | Humorous stories. | CYAC: Crabs—Fiction. | Plankton—Fiction. | Sick—Fiction. | Friendship—Fiction. | Humorous stories. | BISAC: JUVENILE FICTION / Readers / Beginner | JUVENILE FICTION / Social Themes / Friendship | LCGFT: Humorous fiction.

Classification: LCC PZ7.F34843 Ge 2022 | DDC (E)—dc23

LC record available at https://lccn.loc.gov/2021022307

10 9 8 7 6 5 4 3 2 1   22 23 24 25 26

Printed in China   62

First edition, January 2022
Edited by Katie Heit
Book design by Maria Mercado

THE SNIFFLES

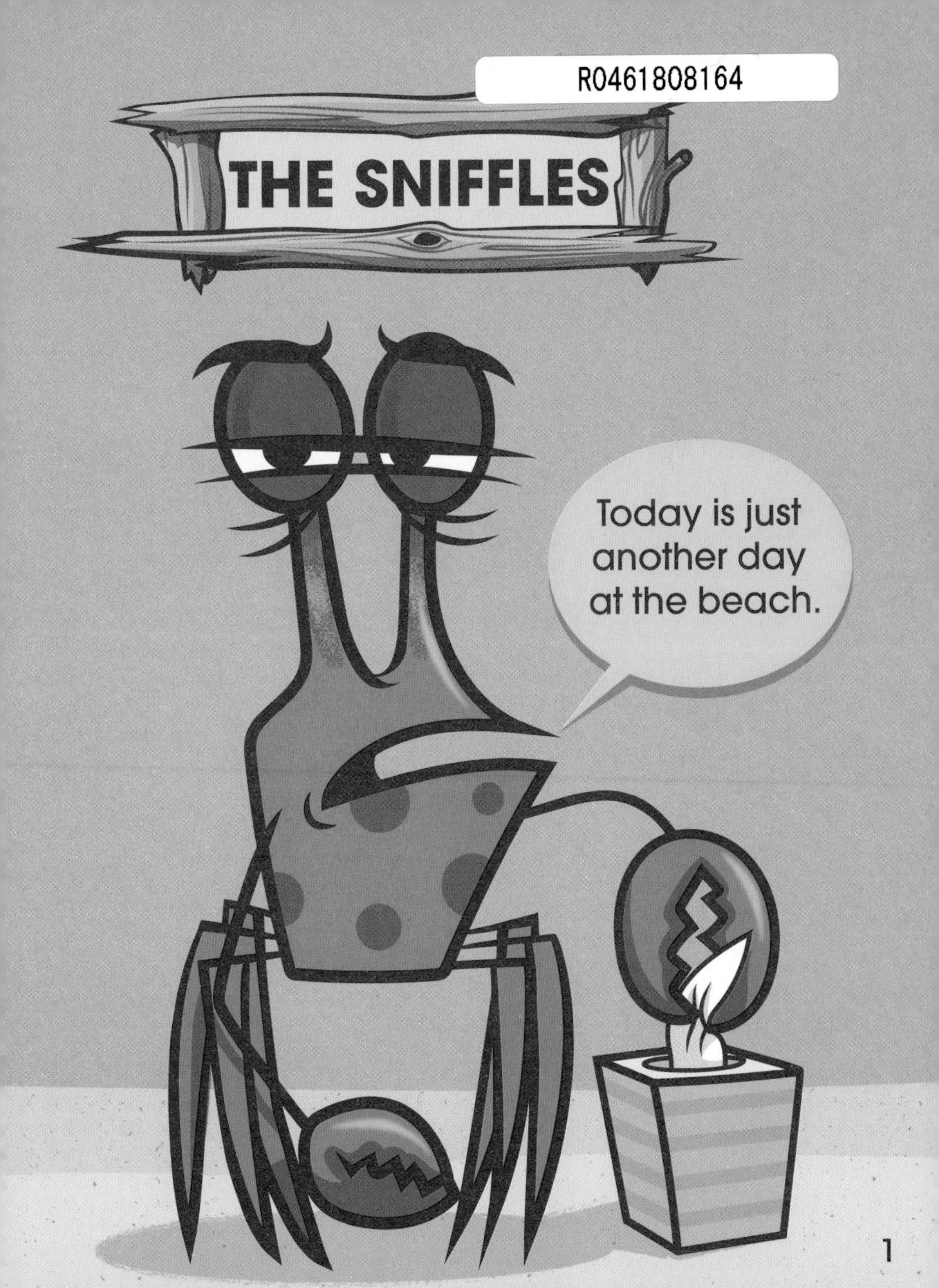
Today is just another day at the beach.

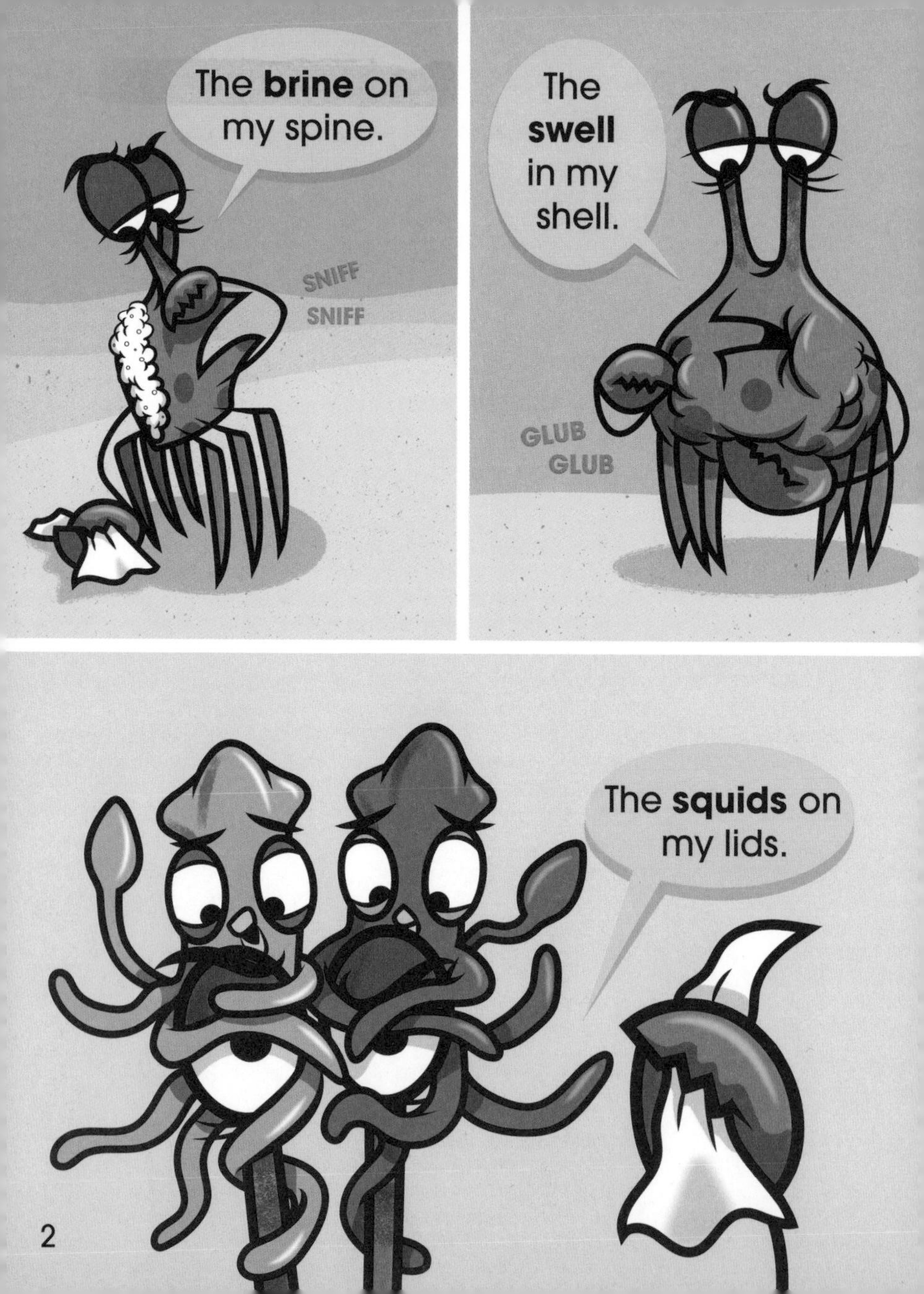
The **brine** on my spine.
SNIFF
SNIFF
The **swell** in my shell.
GLUB
GLUB
The **squids** on my lids.

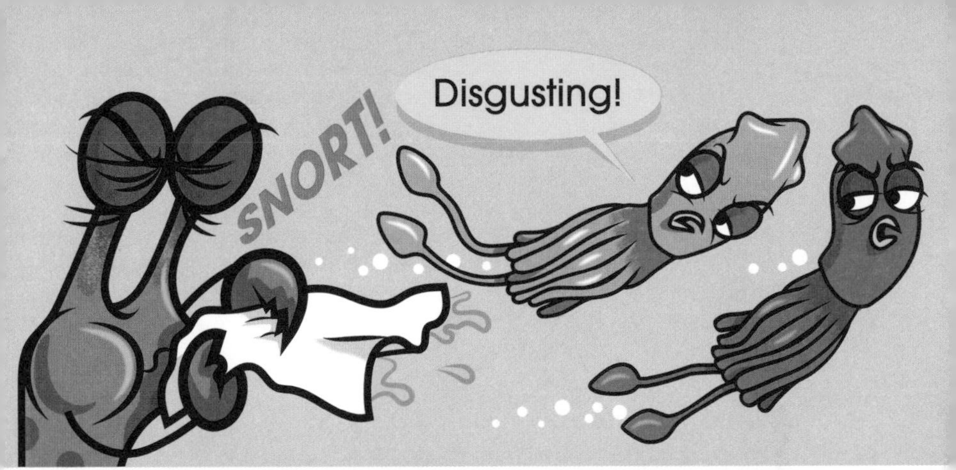
SNORT!
Disgusting!

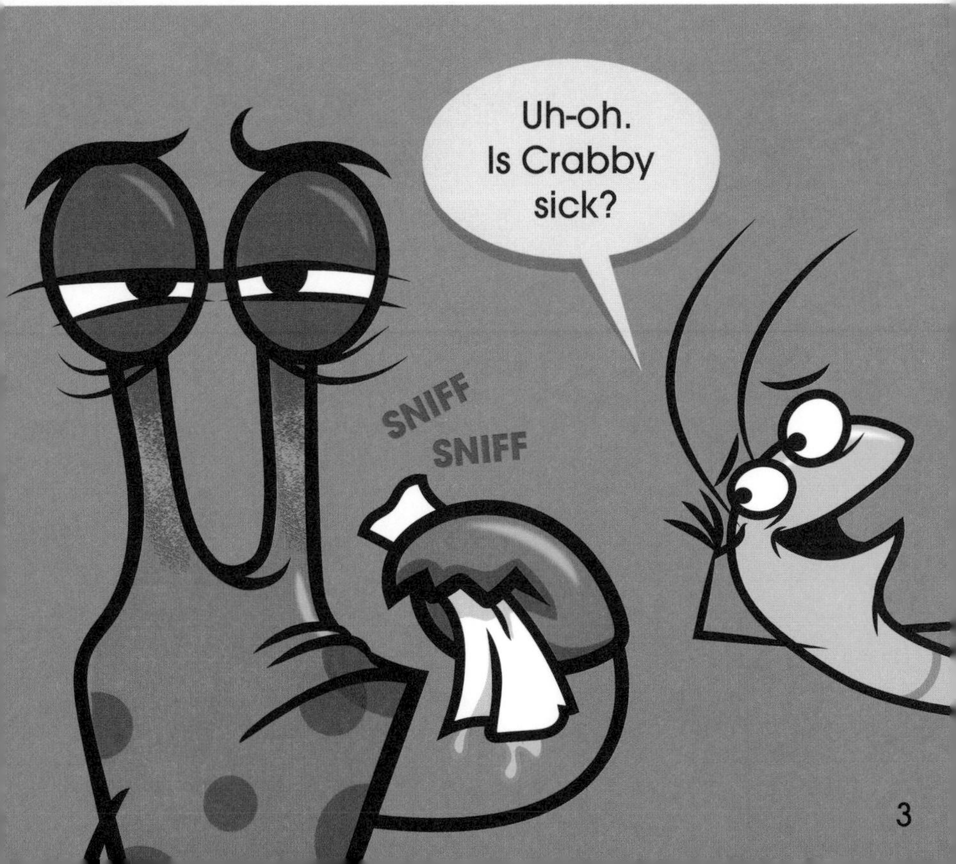
Uh-oh.
Is Crabby
sick?
SNIFF
SNIFF

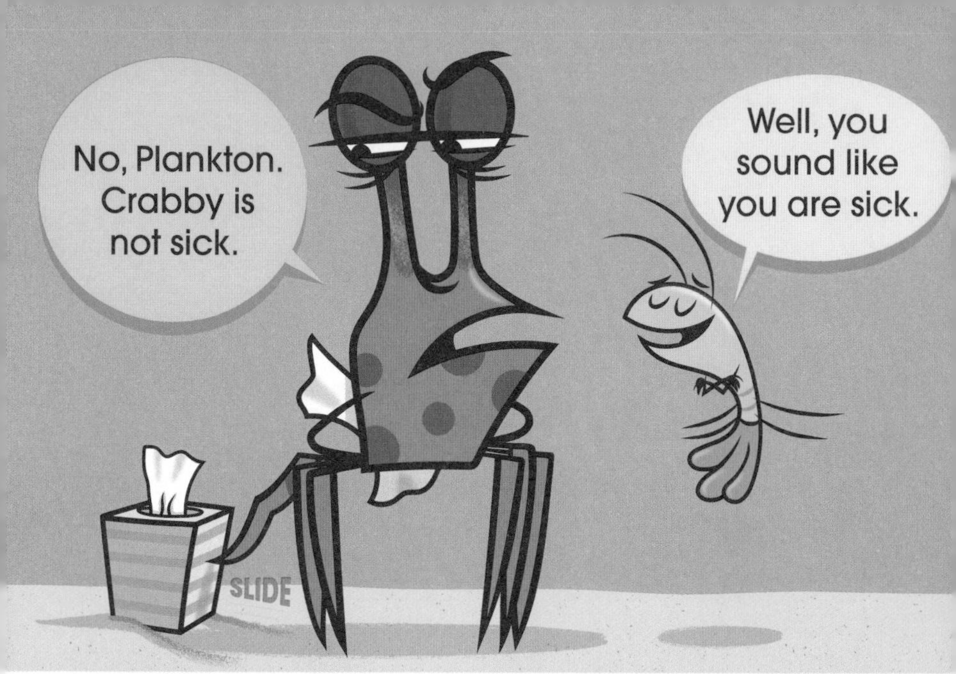
No, Plankton. Crabby is not sick.
Well, you sound like you are sick.
SLIDE

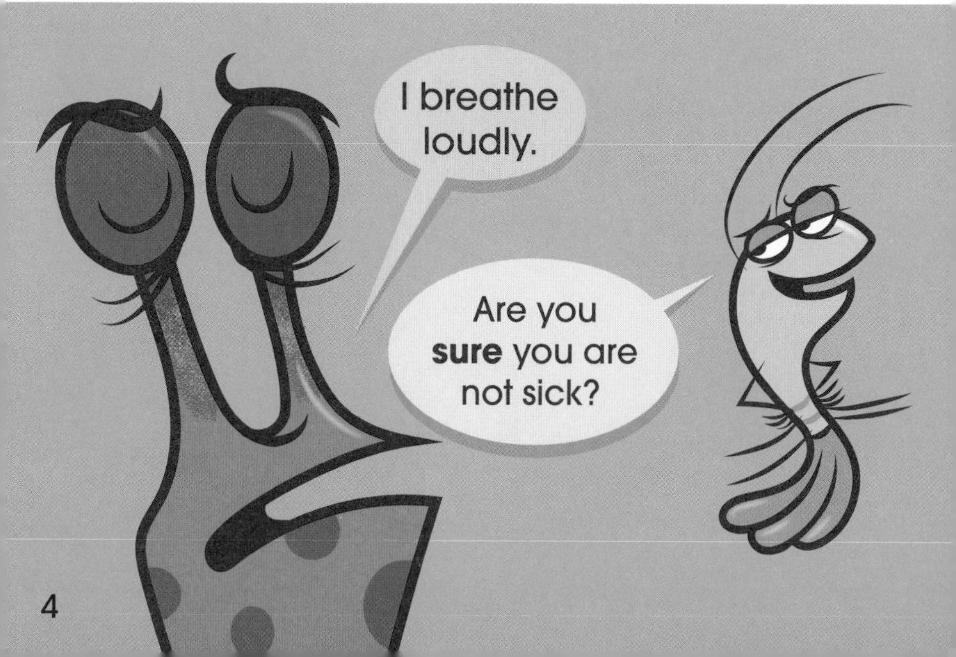
I breathe loudly.
Are you **sure** you are not sick?

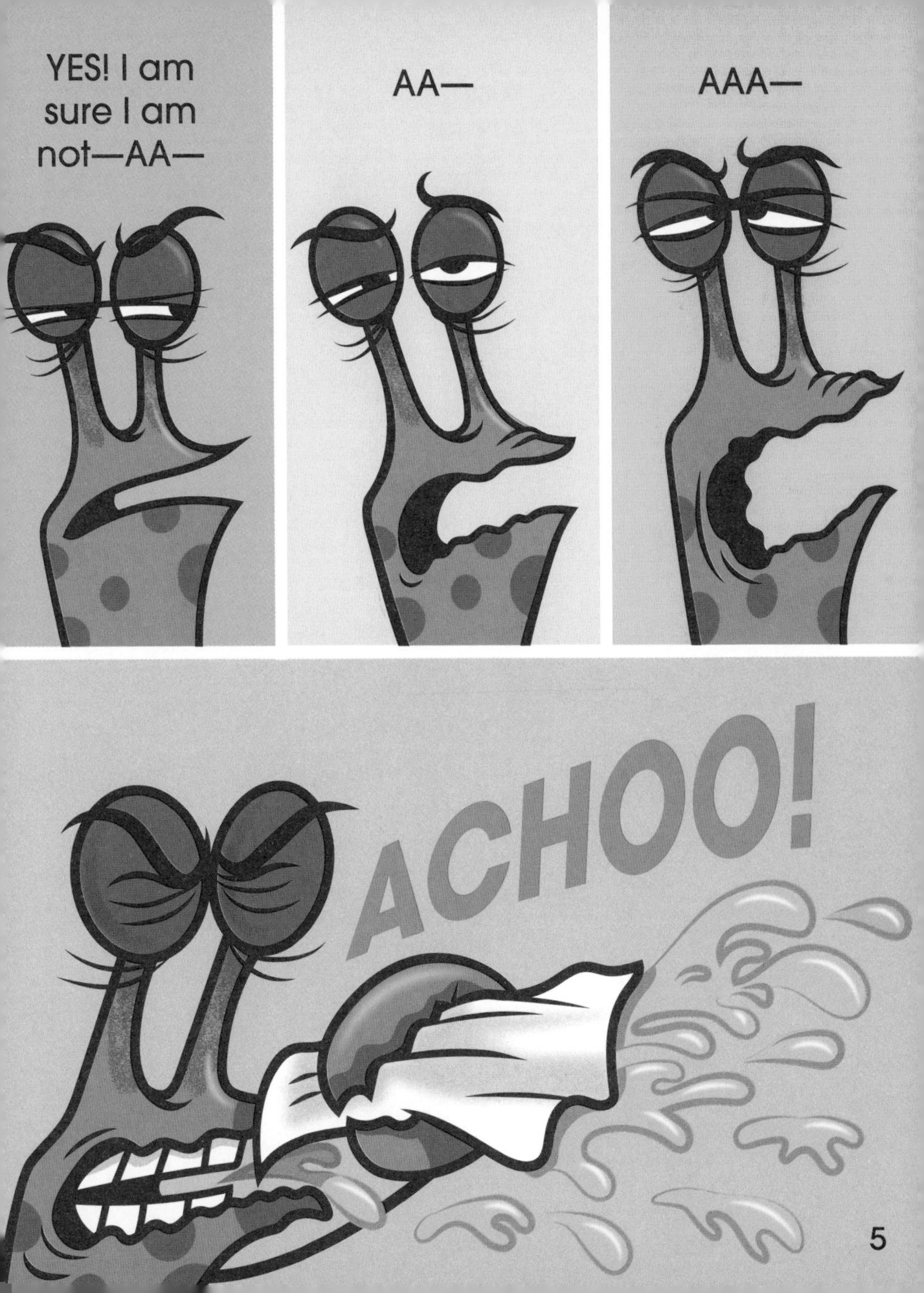
YES! I am sure I am not—AA—
AA—
AAA—
ACHOO!

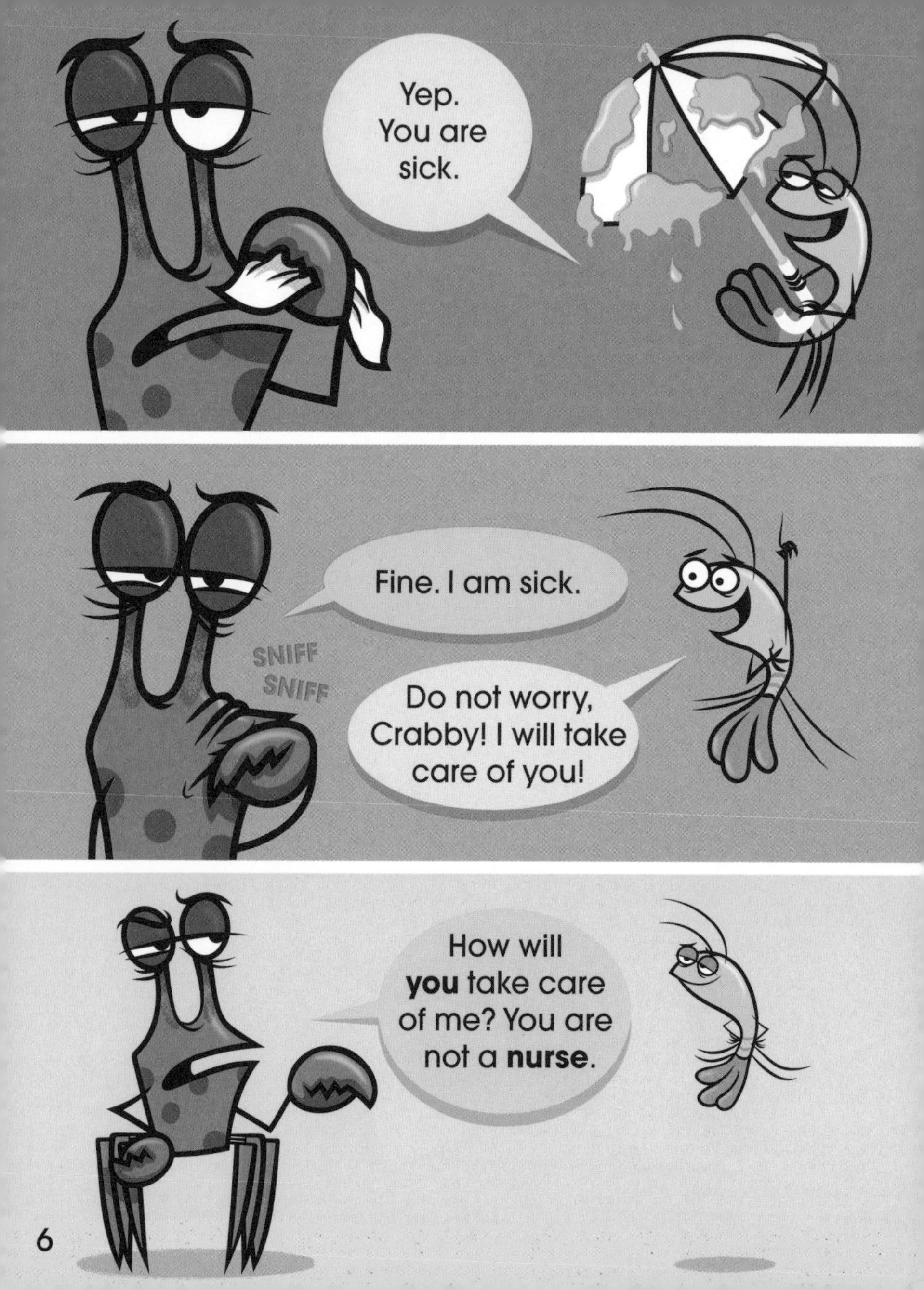
Yep. You are sick.
Fine. I am sick.
SNIFF SNIFF
Do not worry, Crabby! I will take care of you!
How will **you** take care of me? You are not a **nurse**.

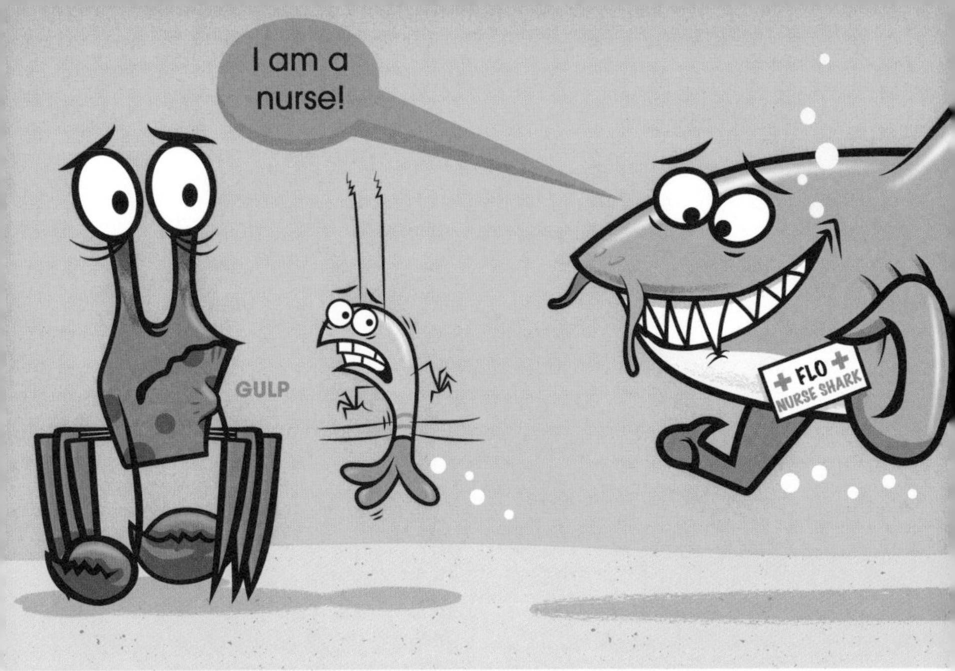
I am a nurse!
GULP
FLO
NURSE SHARK

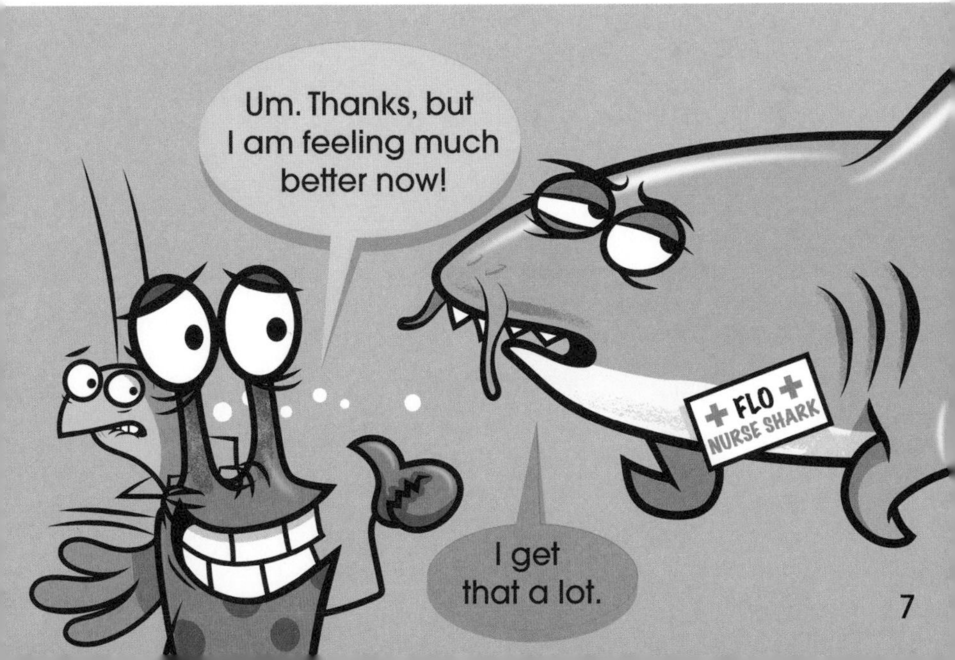
Um. Thanks, but I am feeling much better now!
FLO
NURSE SHARK
I get that a lot.

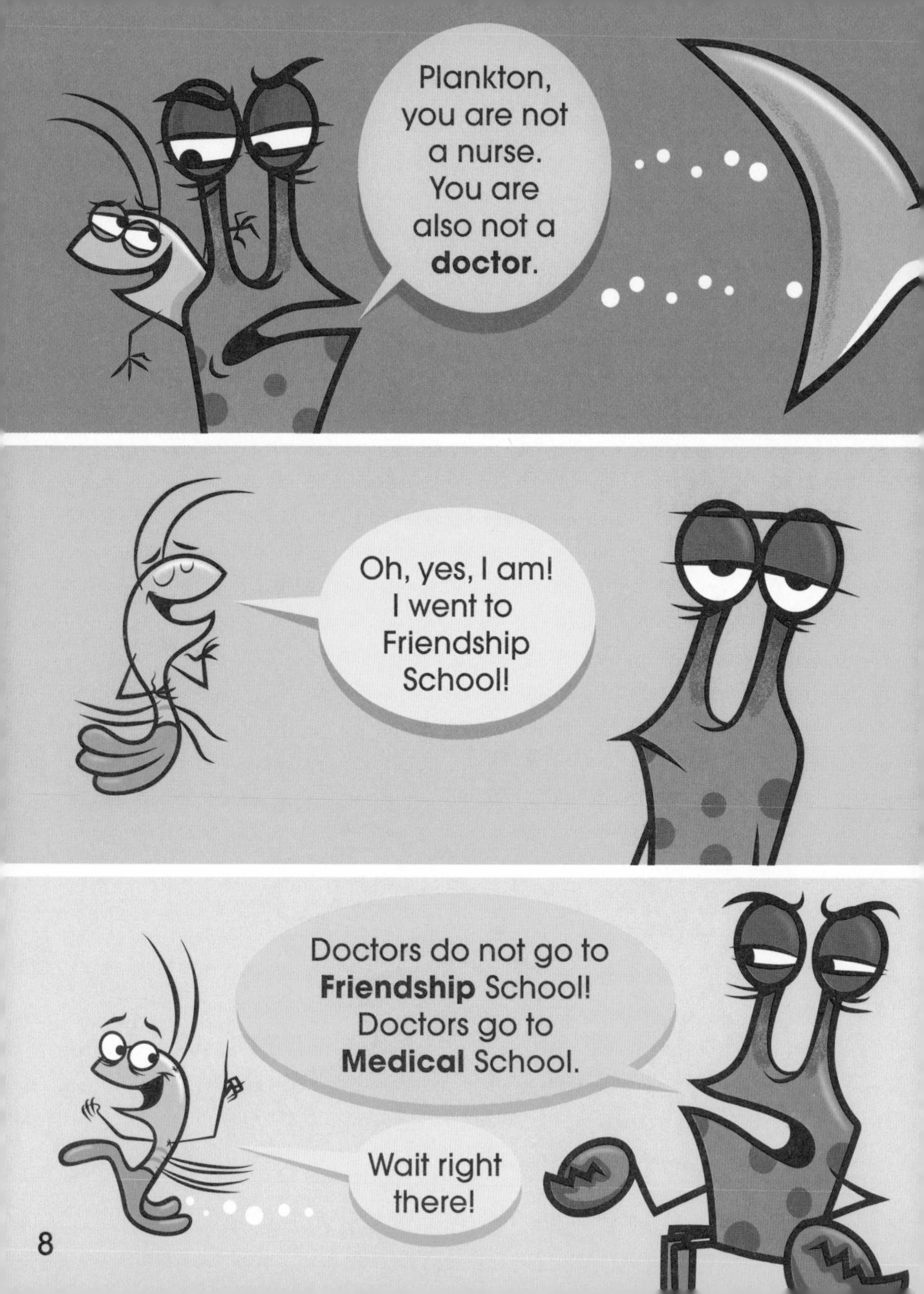
Plankton, you are not a nurse. You are also not a **doctor**.
Oh, yes, I am! I went to Friendship School!
Doctors do not go to **Friendship** School! Doctors go to **Medical** School.
Wait right there!

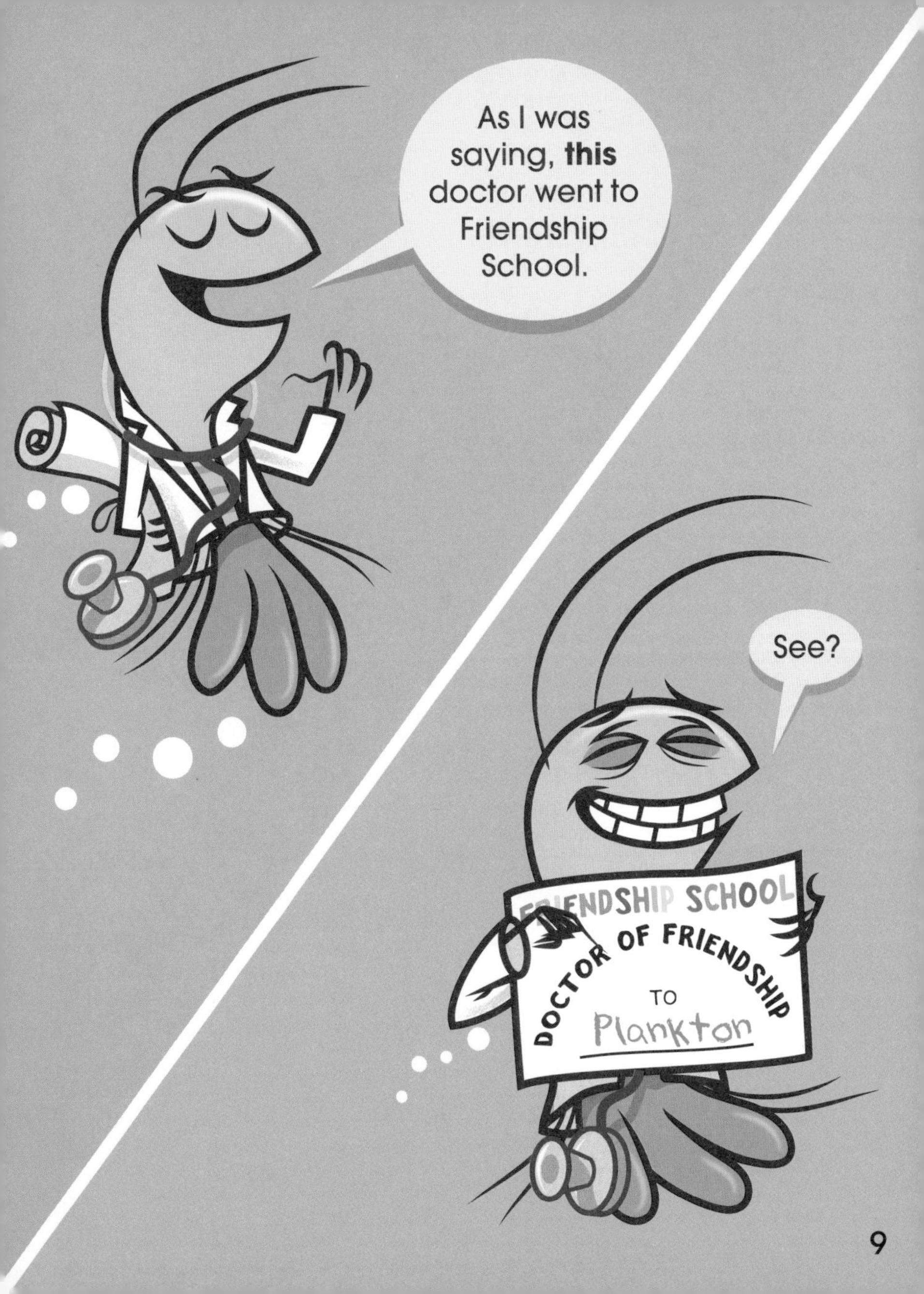
As I was saying, **this** doctor went to Friendship School.
See?
FRIENDSHIP SCHOOL
DOCTOR OF FRIENDSHIP
TO
Plankton

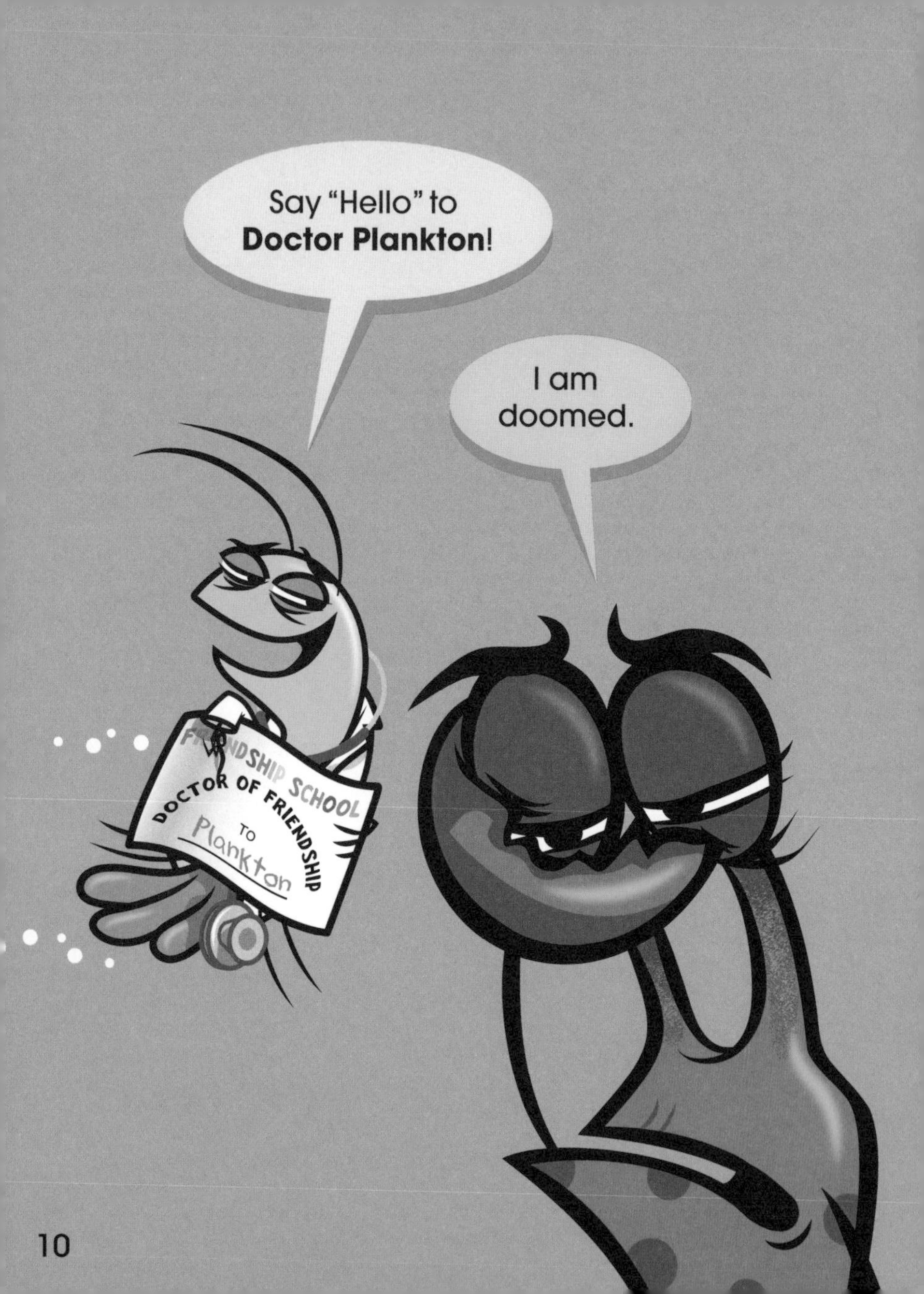
Say "Hello" to **Doctor Plankton**!
I am doomed.
FRIENDSHIP SCHOOL
DOCTOR OF FRIENDSHIP
TO
Plankton

THE FEVER

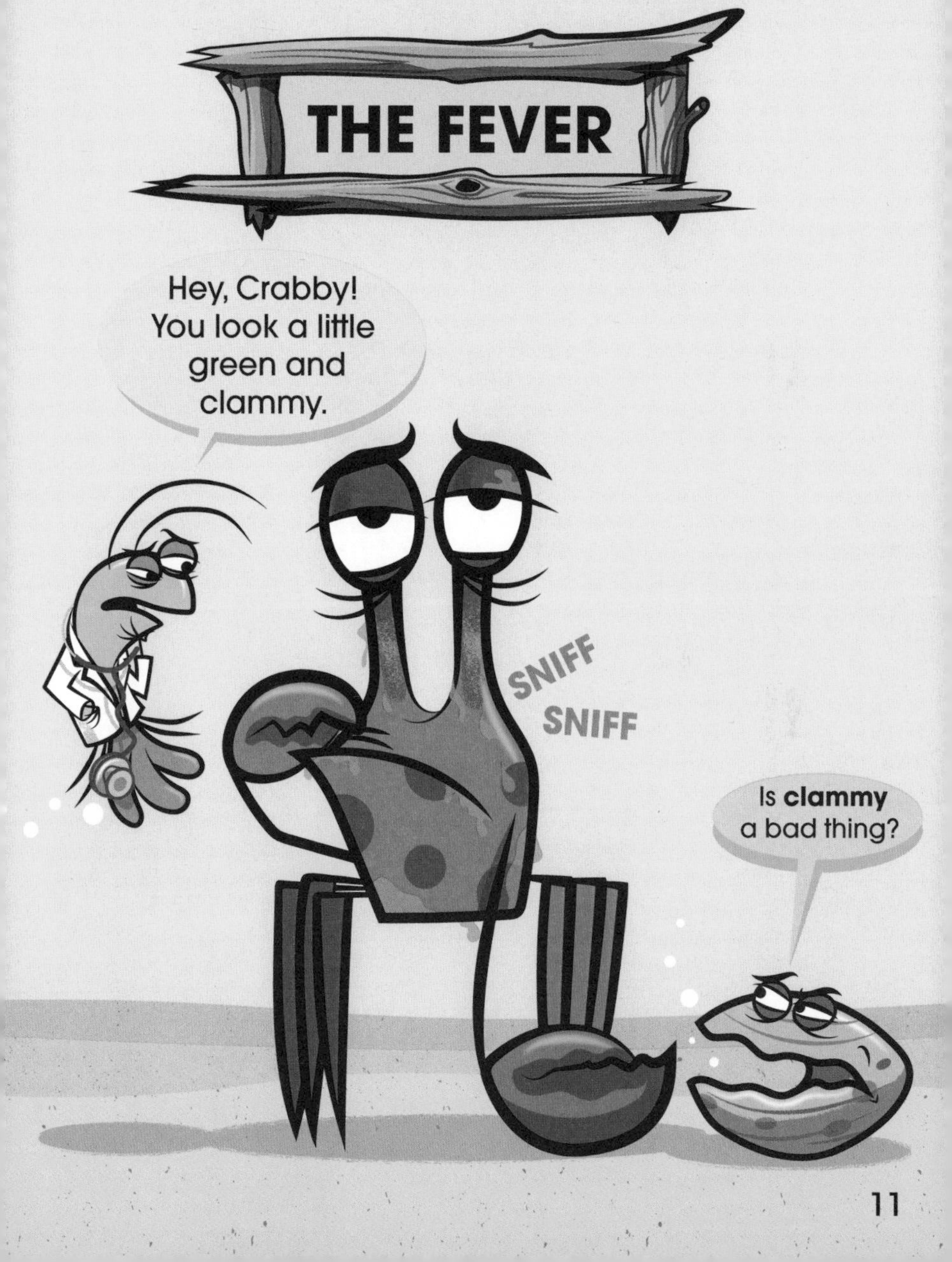
Hey, Crabby! You look a little green and clammy.
SNIFF
SNIFF
Is **clammy** a bad thing?

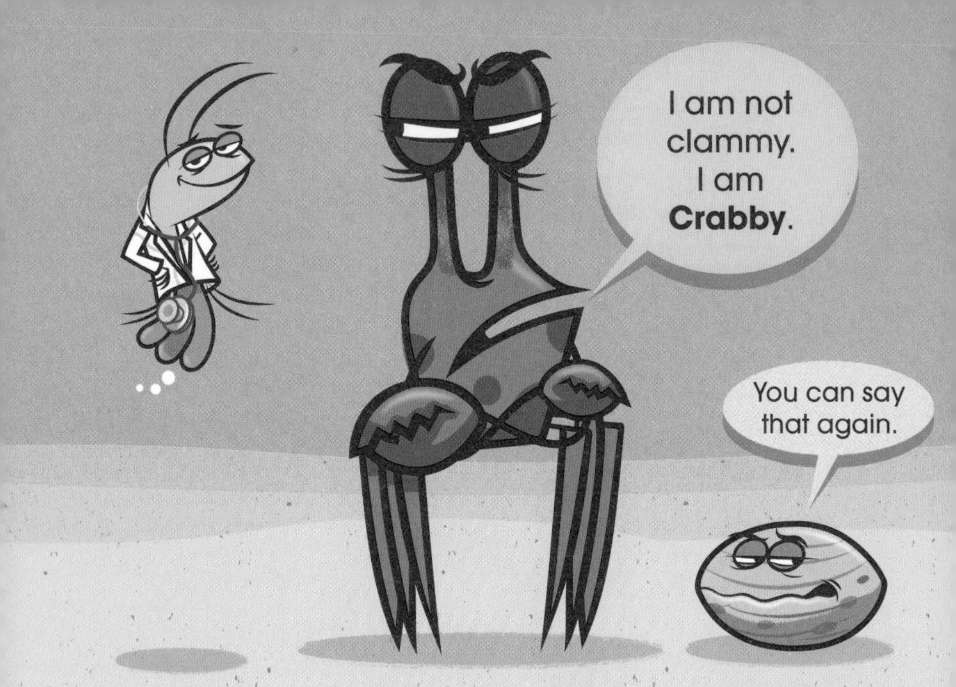
I am not clammy. I am **Crabby**.
You can say that again.

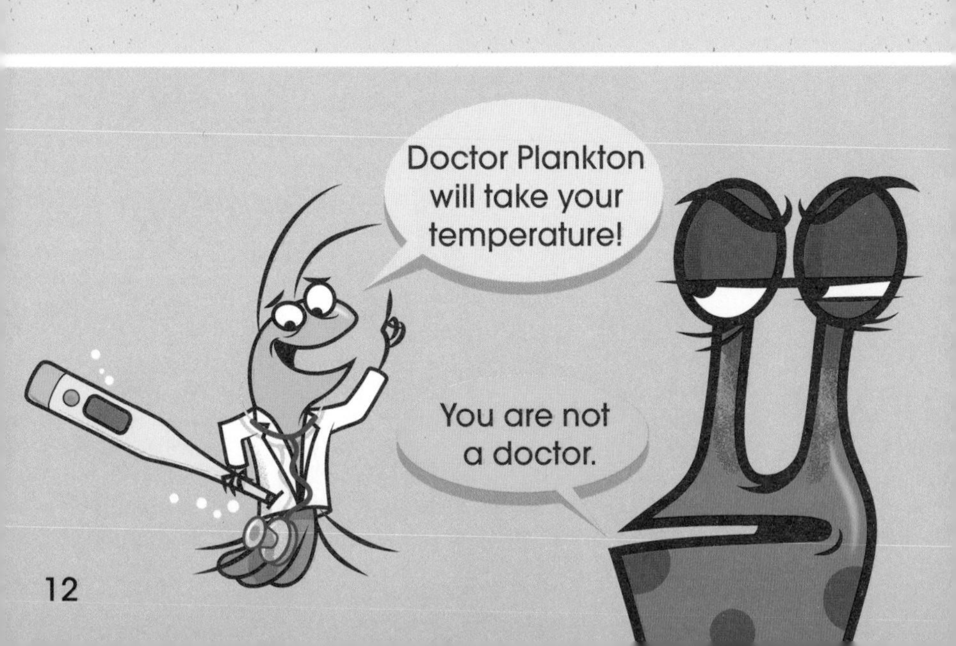
Doctor Plankton will take your temperature!
You are not a doctor.

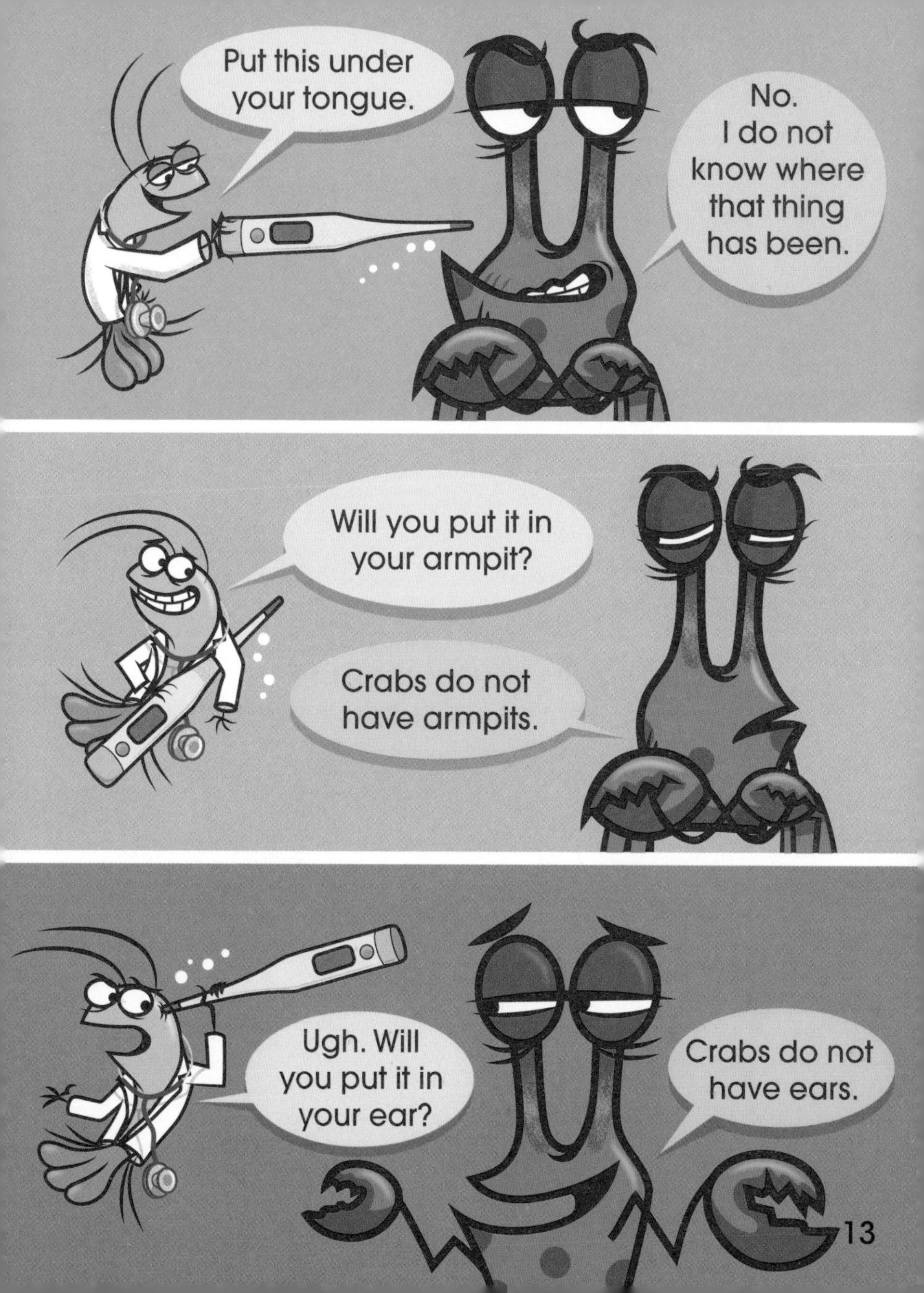
Put this under your tongue.
No. I do not know where that thing has been.
Will you put it in your armpit?
Crabs do not have armpits.
Ugh. Will you put it in your ear?
Crabs do not have ears.

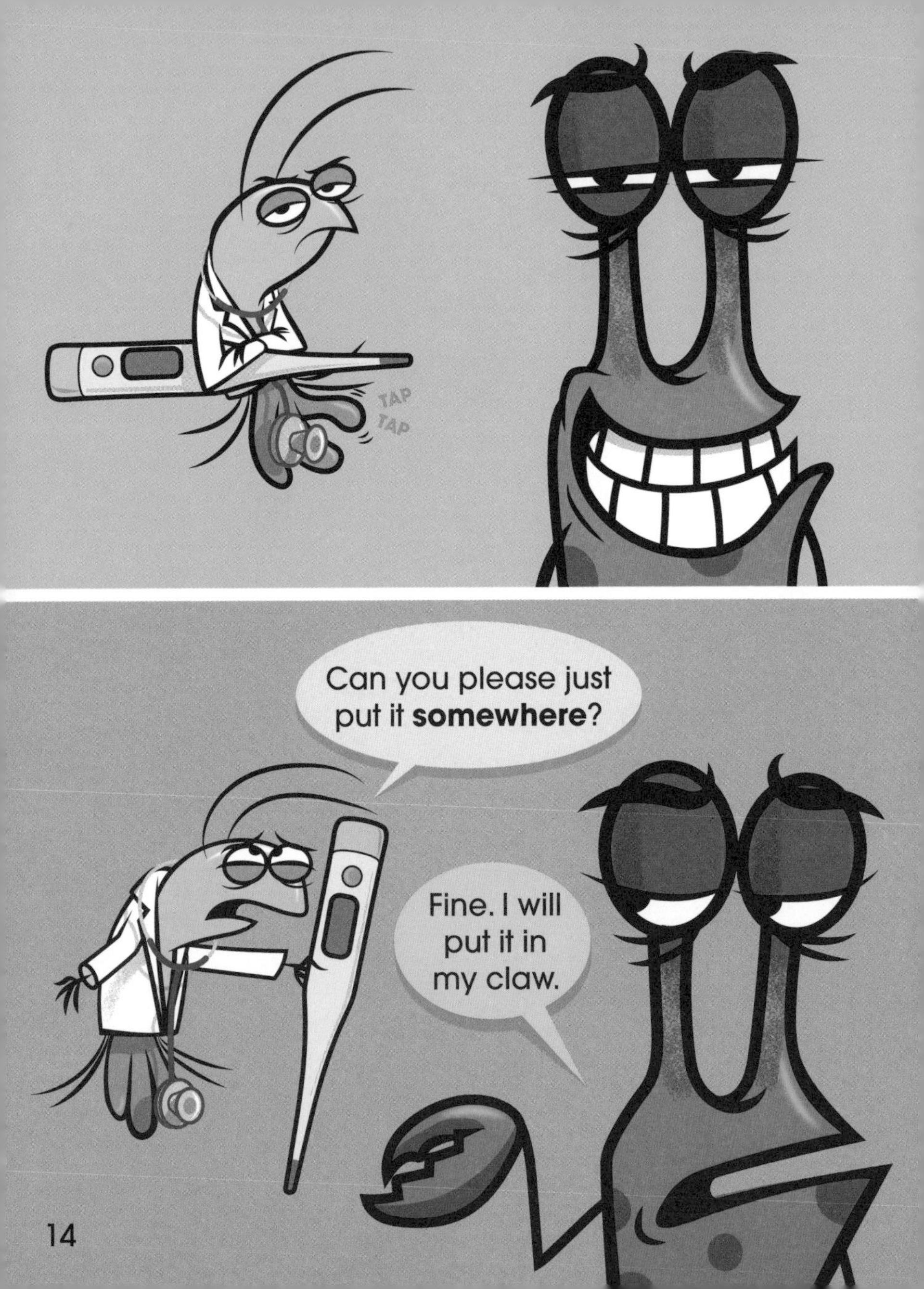
TAP
TAP
Can you please just put it **somewhere**?
Fine. I will put it in my claw.

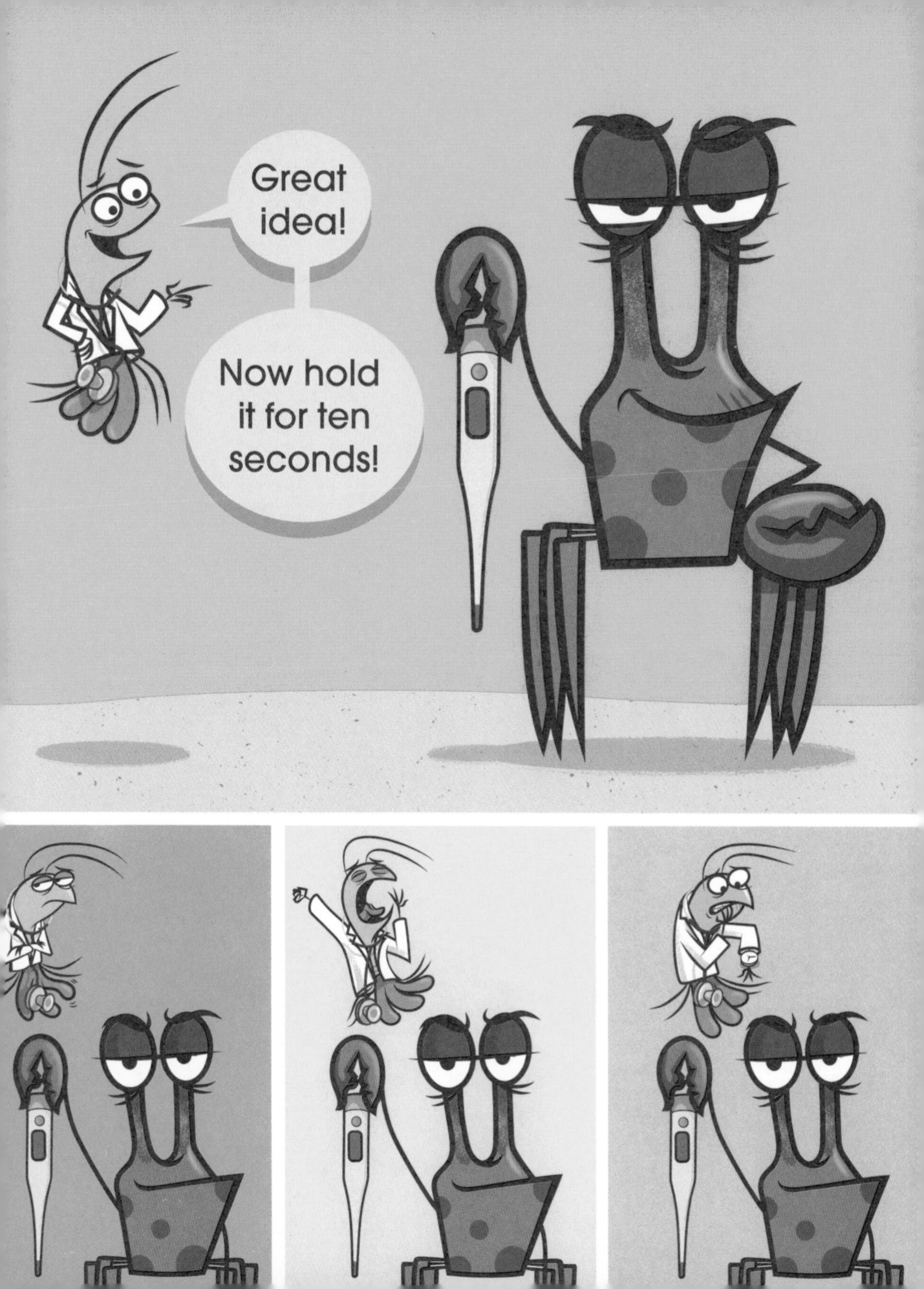
Great idea!
Now hold it for ten seconds!

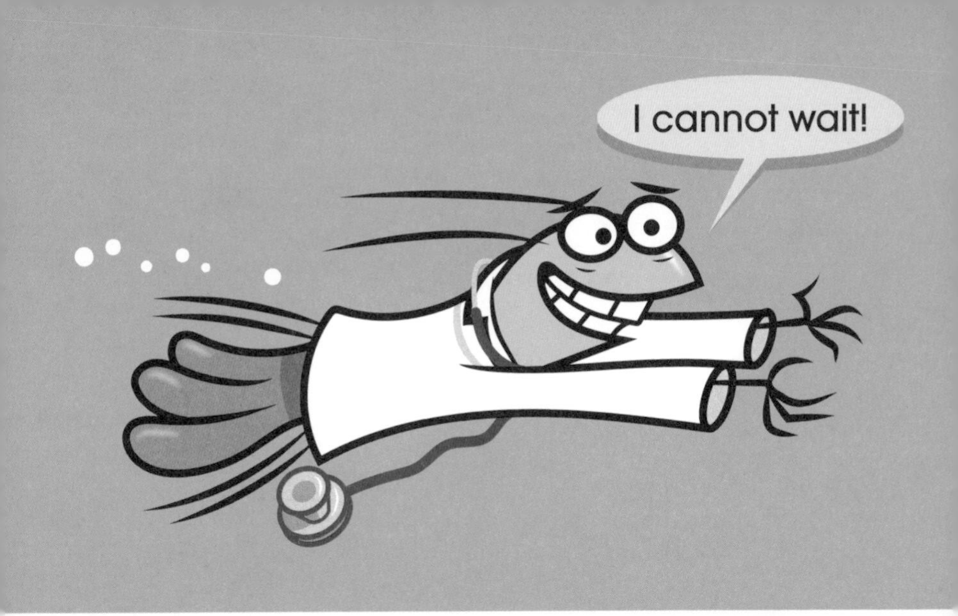
I cannot wait!

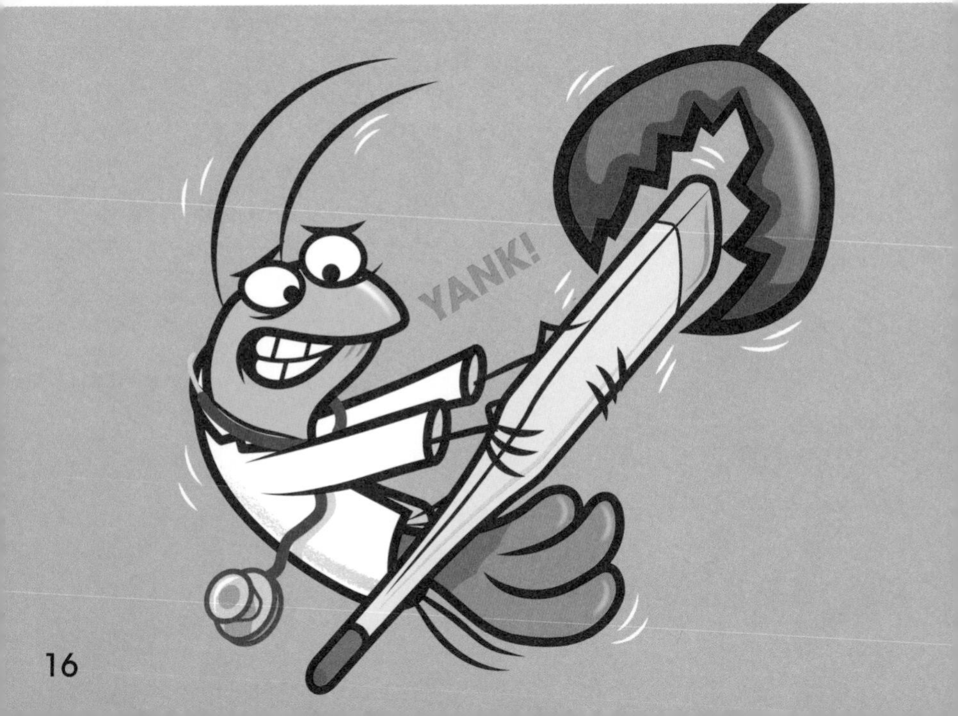
YANK!

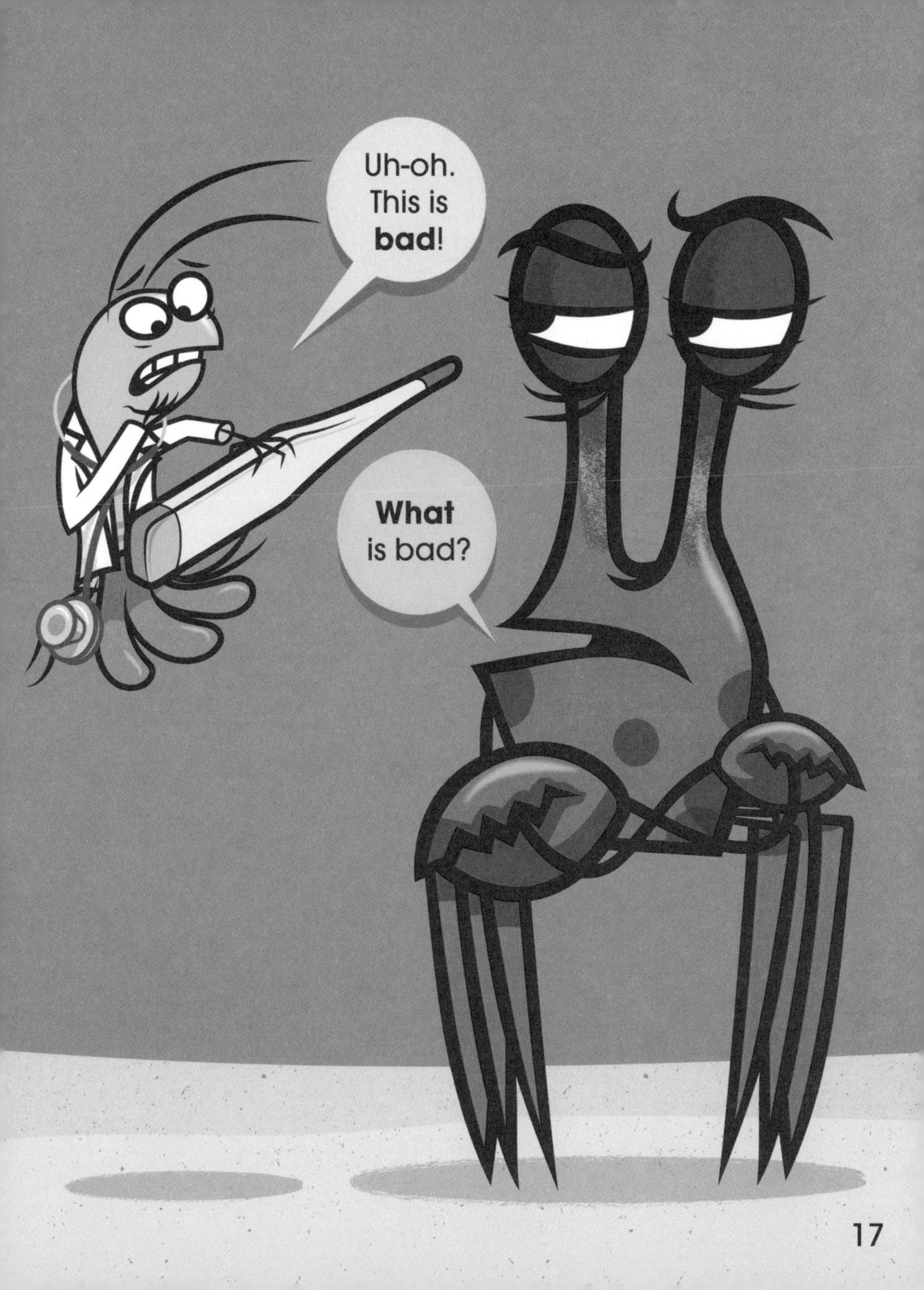
Uh-oh. This is **bad**!
What is bad?

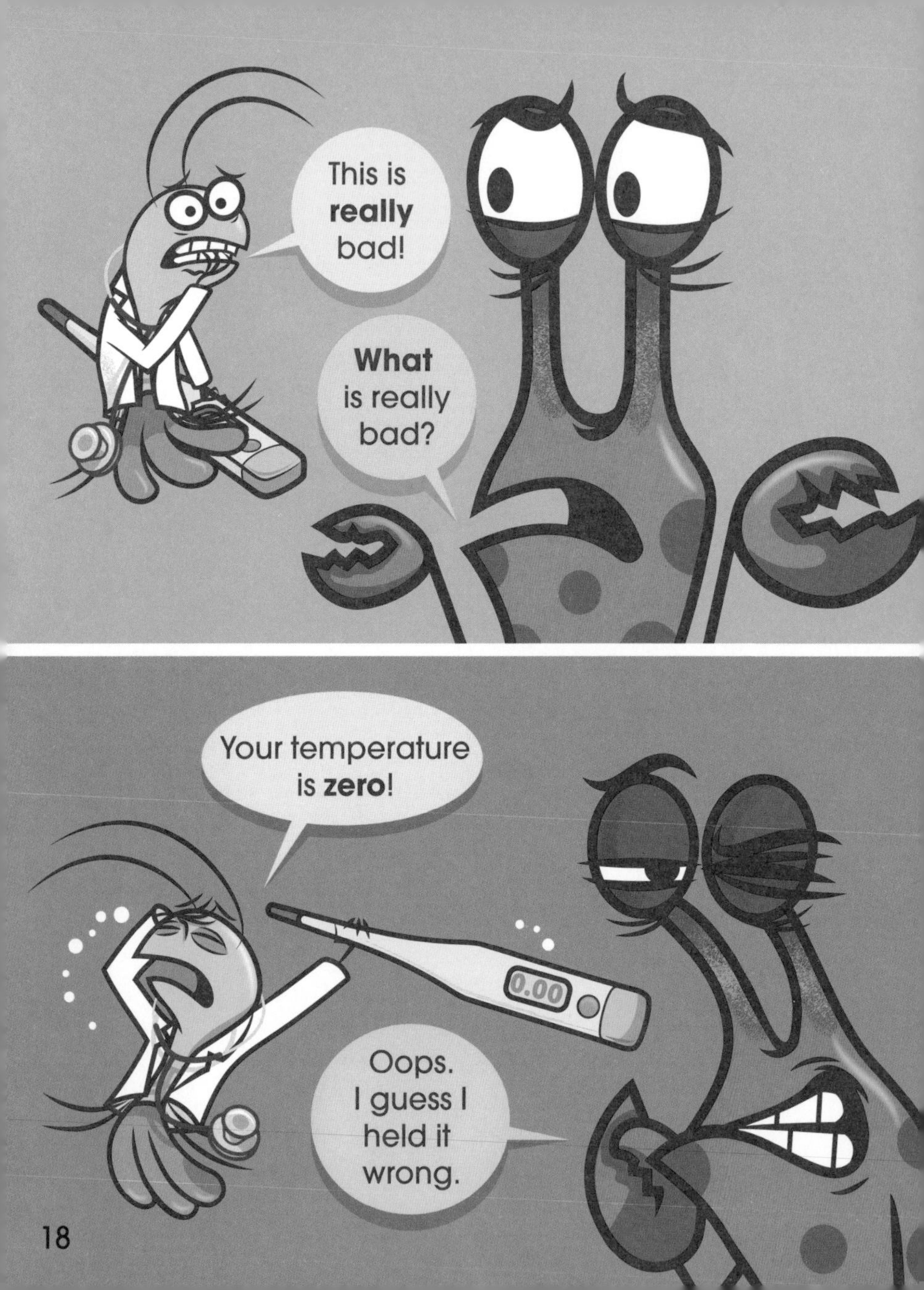
This is **really** bad!
What is really bad?
Your temperature is **zero**!
0.00
Oops. I guess I held it wrong.

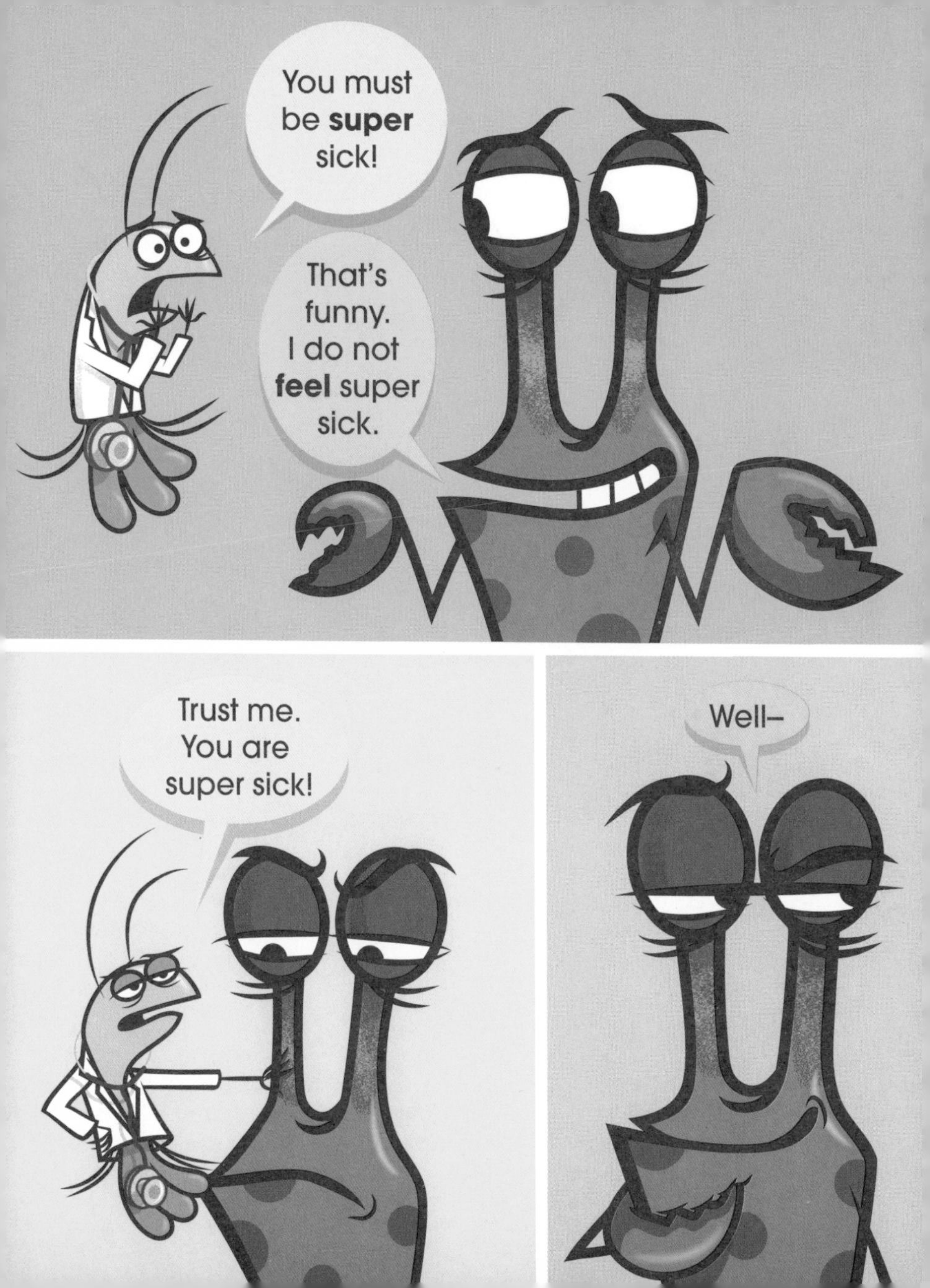
You must be **super** sick!
That's funny. I do not **feel** super sick.
Trust me. You are super sick!
Well–

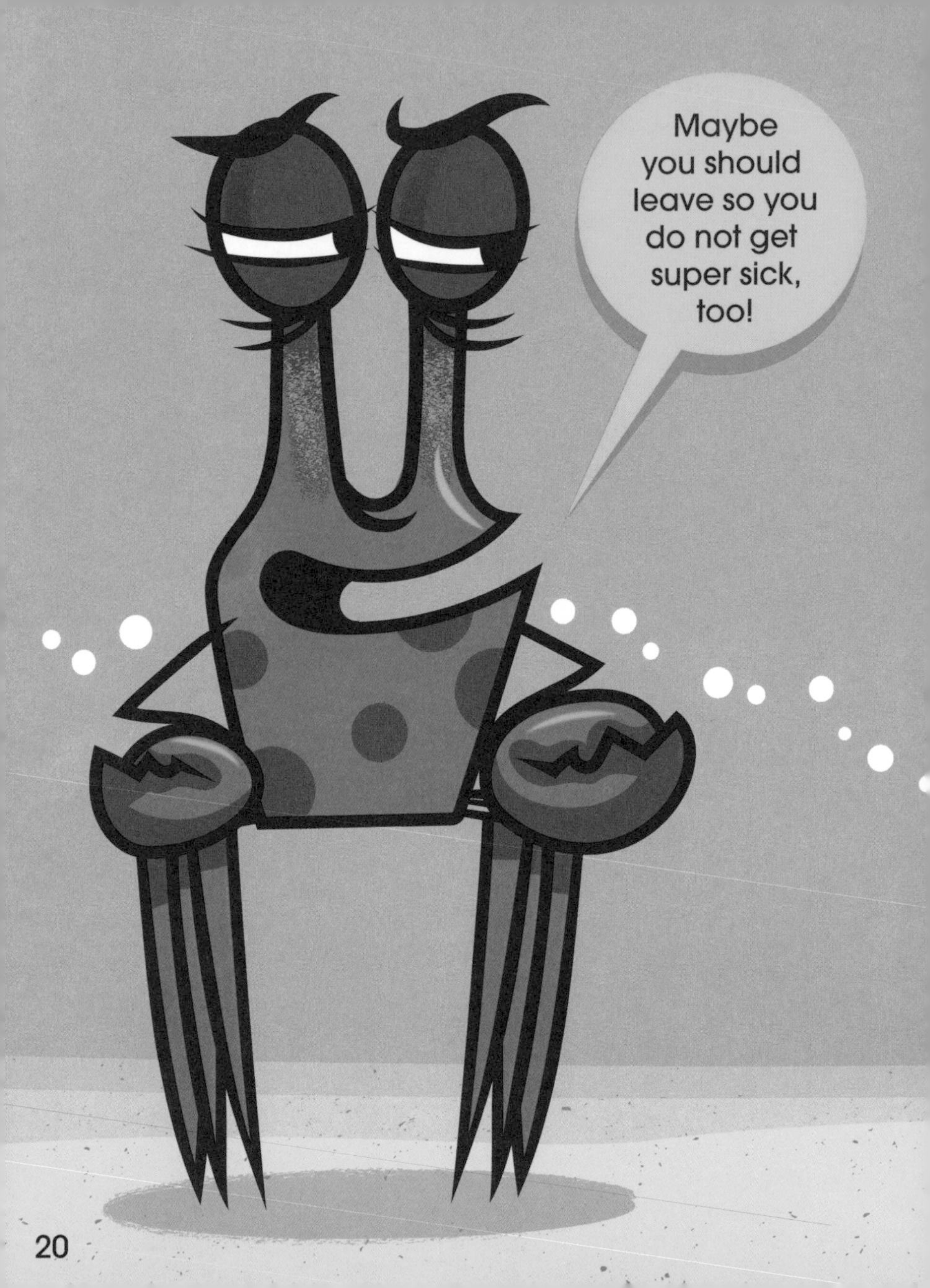
Maybe you should leave so you do not get super sick, too!

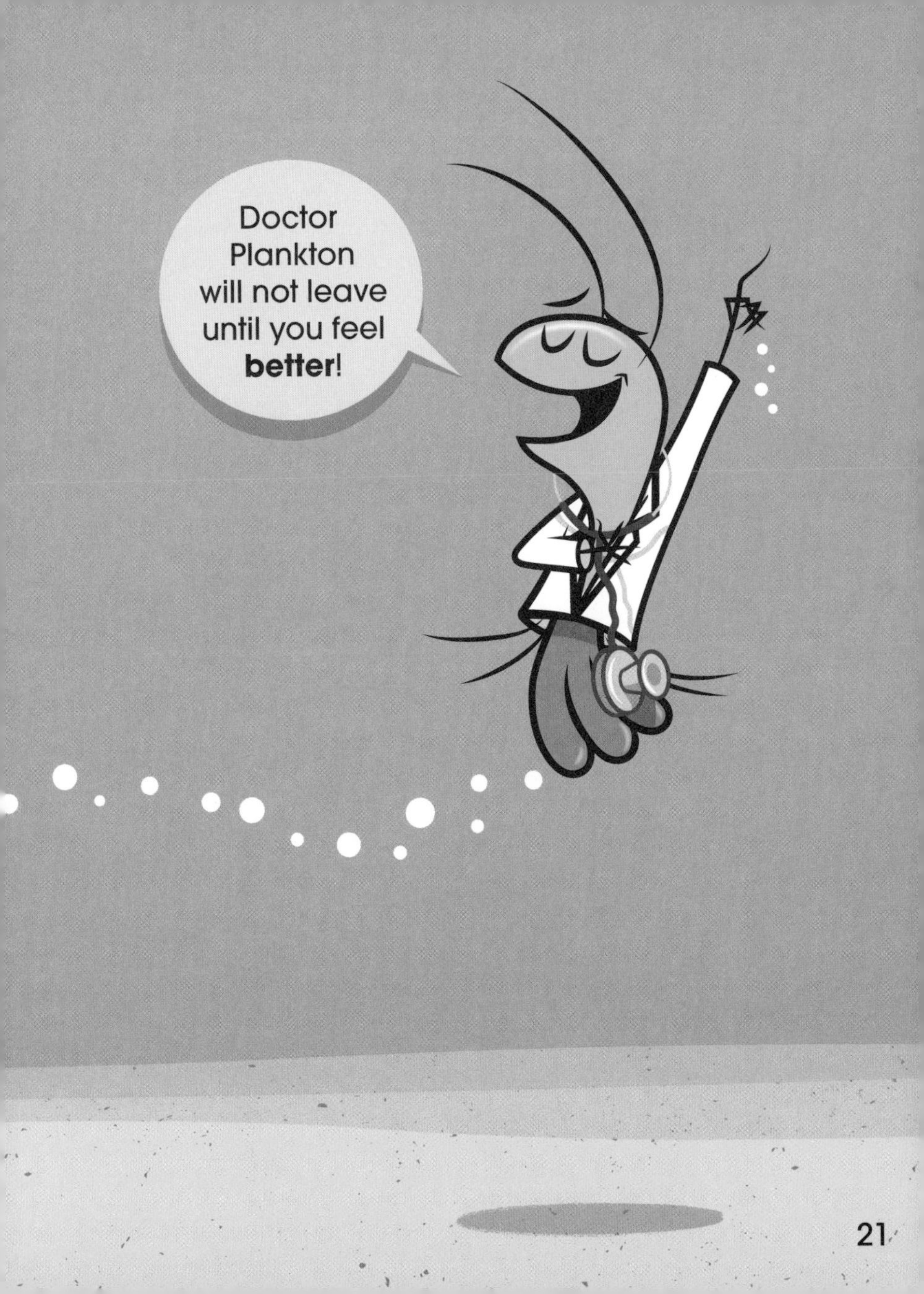
Doctor Plankton will not leave until you feel **better**!

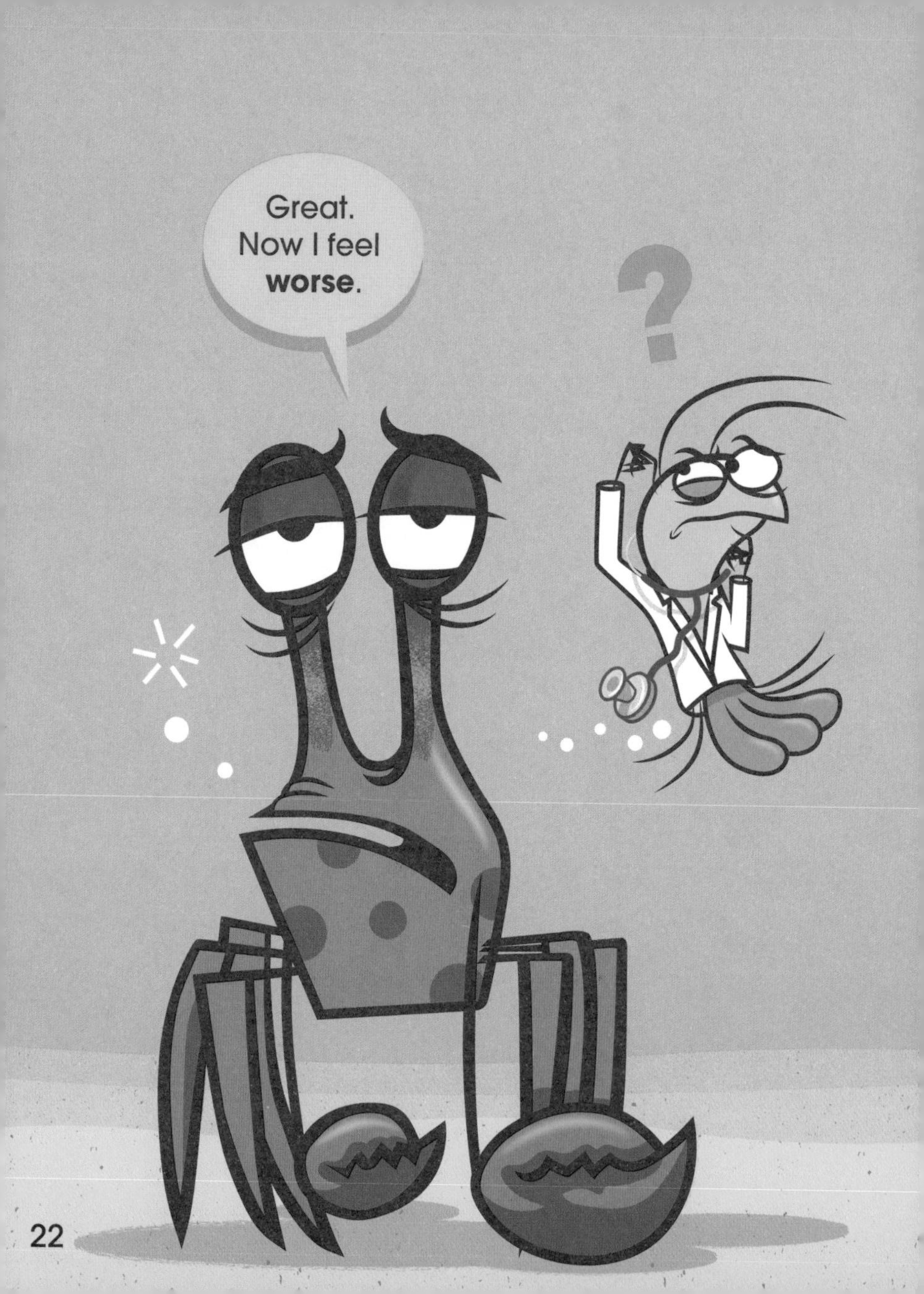
Great.
Now I feel
worse.
?

THE BANDAGE

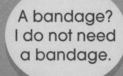

This bandage should fix you up, Crabby!

A bandage? I do not need a bandage.

SNIFF SNIFF

23

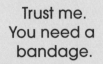
Trust me. You need a bandage.

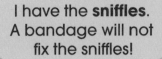
I have the **sniffles**. A bandage will not fix the sniffles!

Excuse me. Who is the doctor here?

You are **not** a doctor.

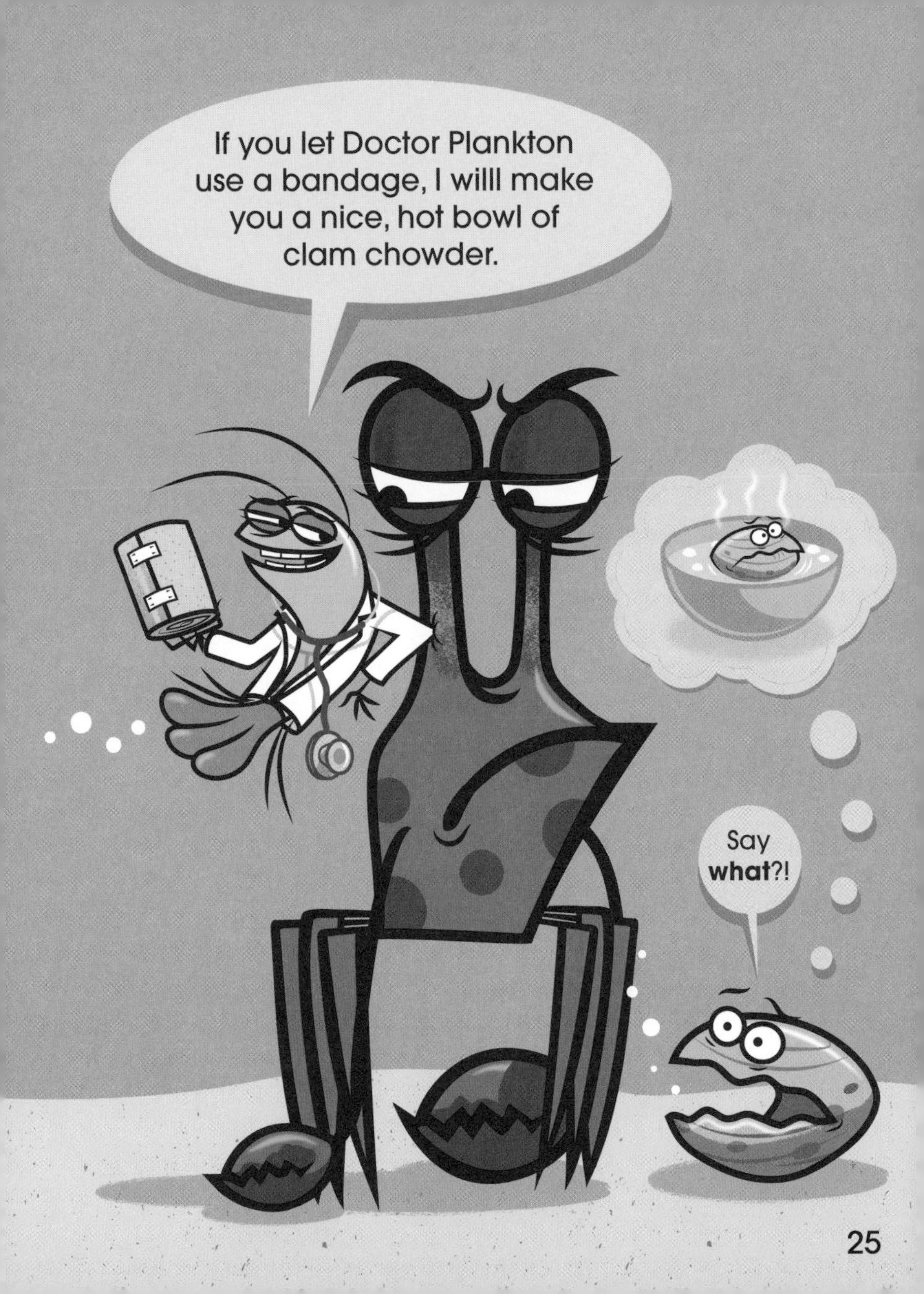
If you let Doctor Plankton use a bandage, I willl make you a nice, hot bowl of clam chowder.
Say **what**?!

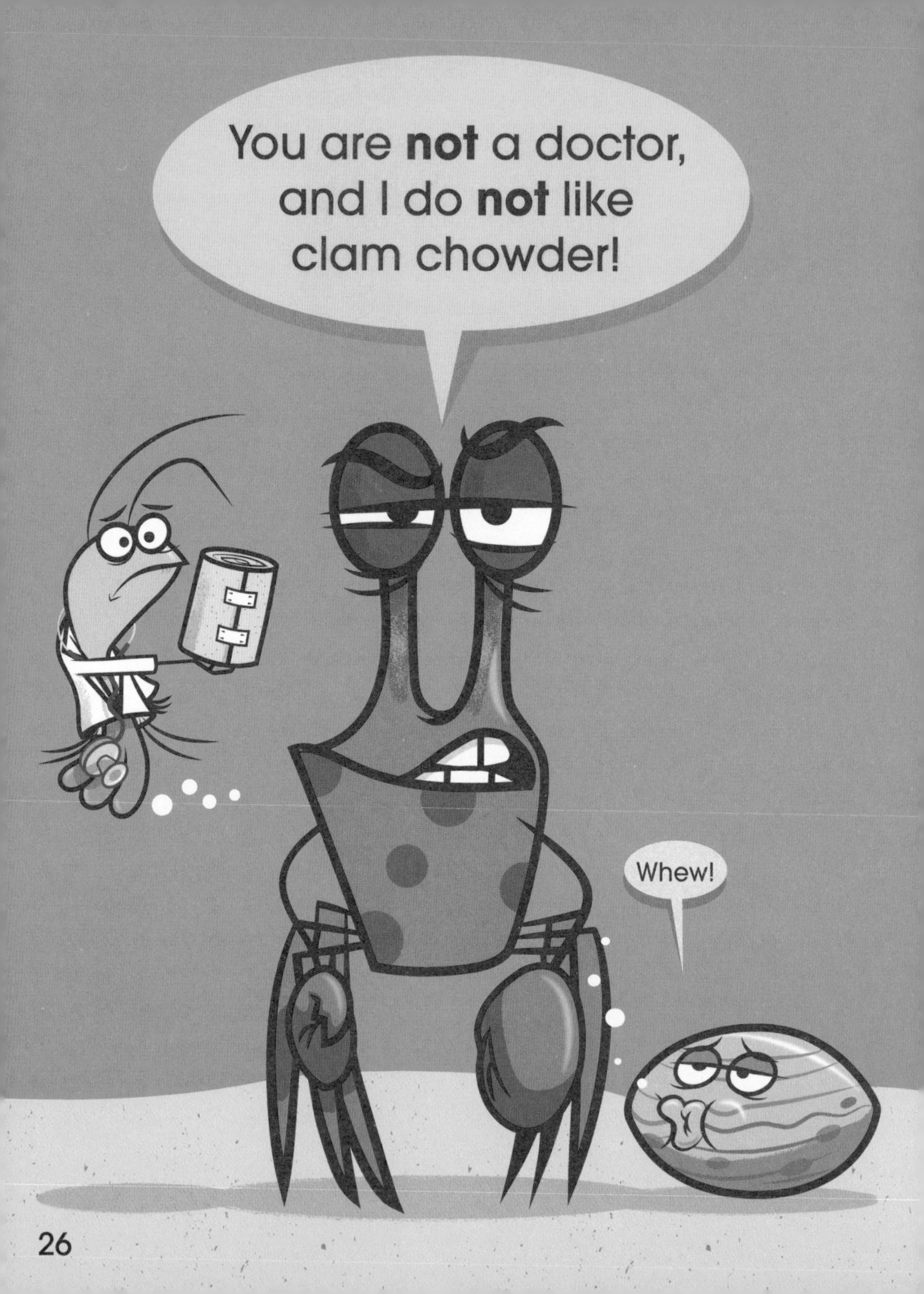
You are **not** a doctor, and I do **not** like clam chowder!
Whew!

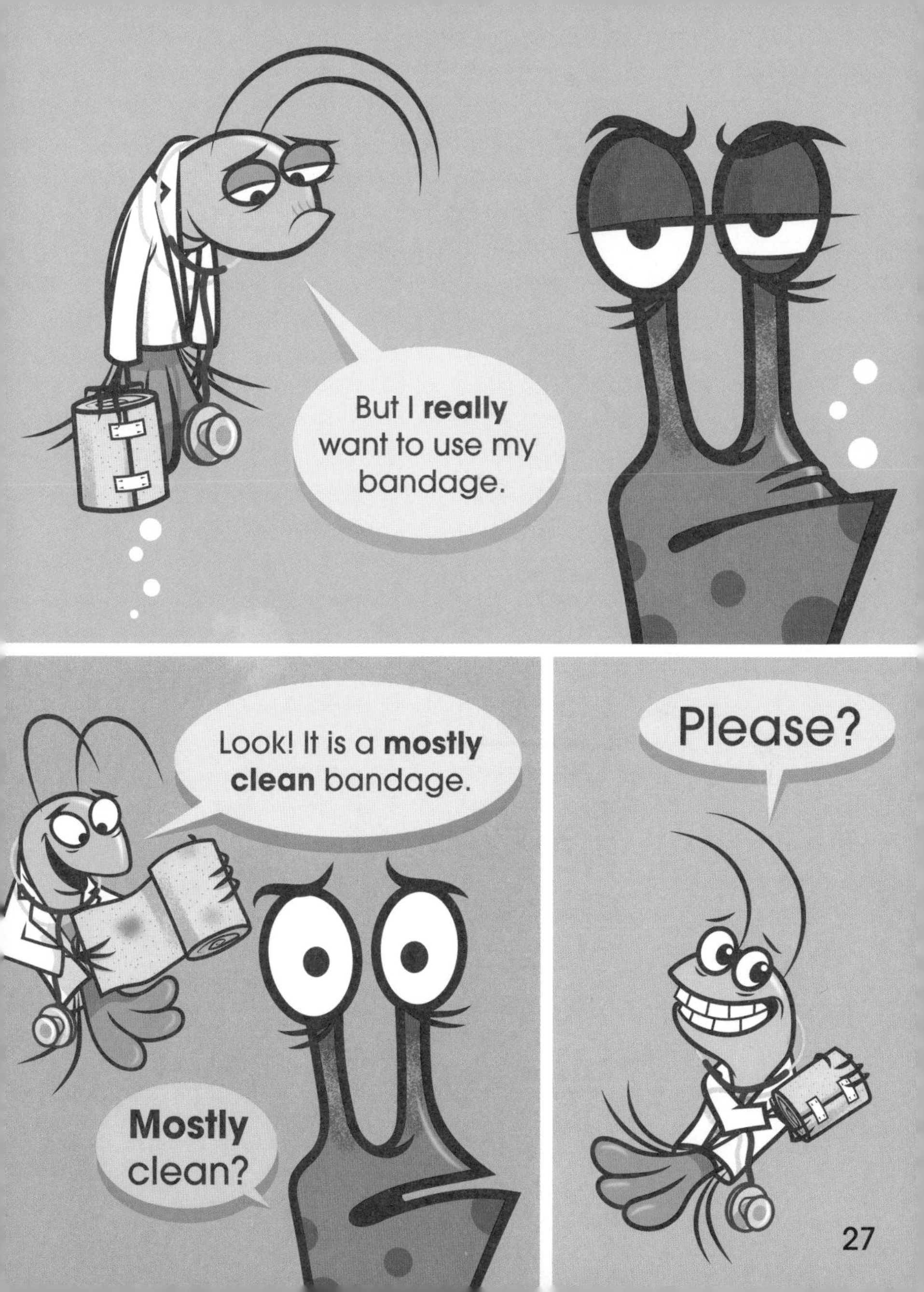
But I **really** want to use my bandage.
Look! It is a **mostly clean** bandage.
Mostly clean?
Please?

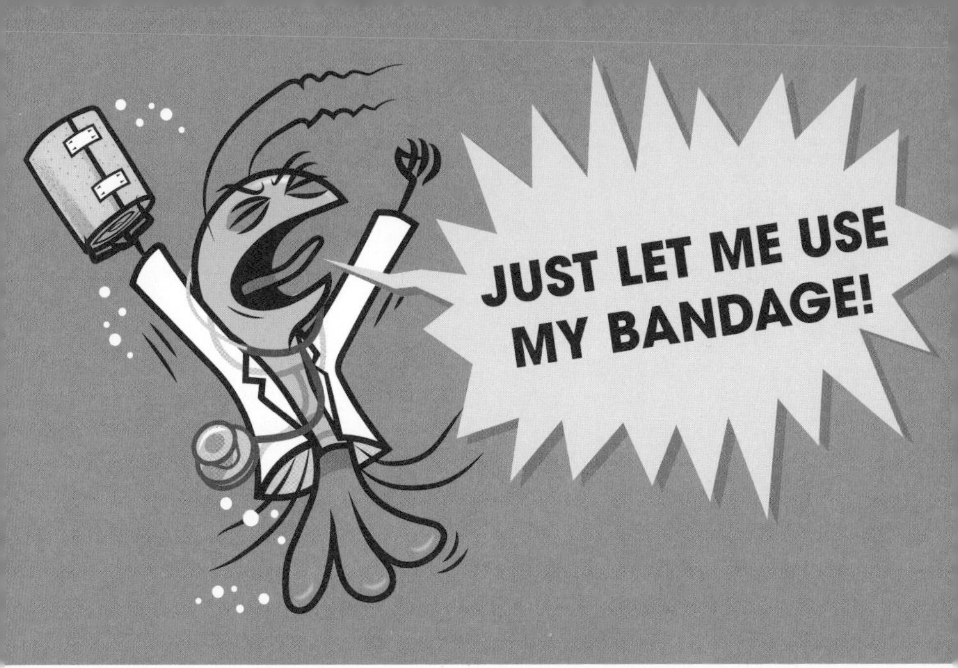
JUST LET ME USE MY BANDAGE!

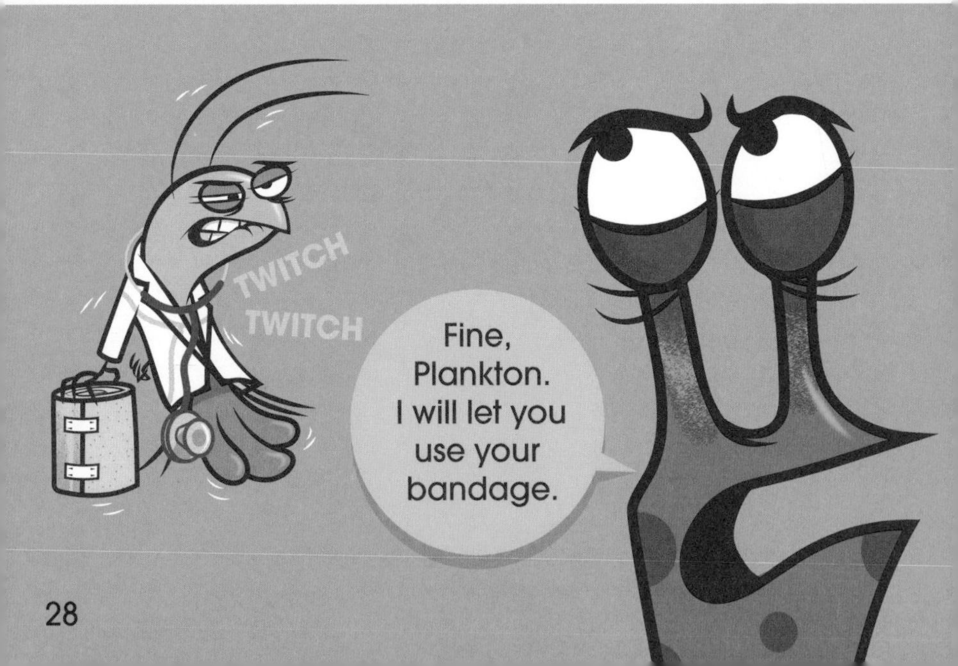
TWITCH
TWITCH
Fine, Plankton. I will let you use your bandage.

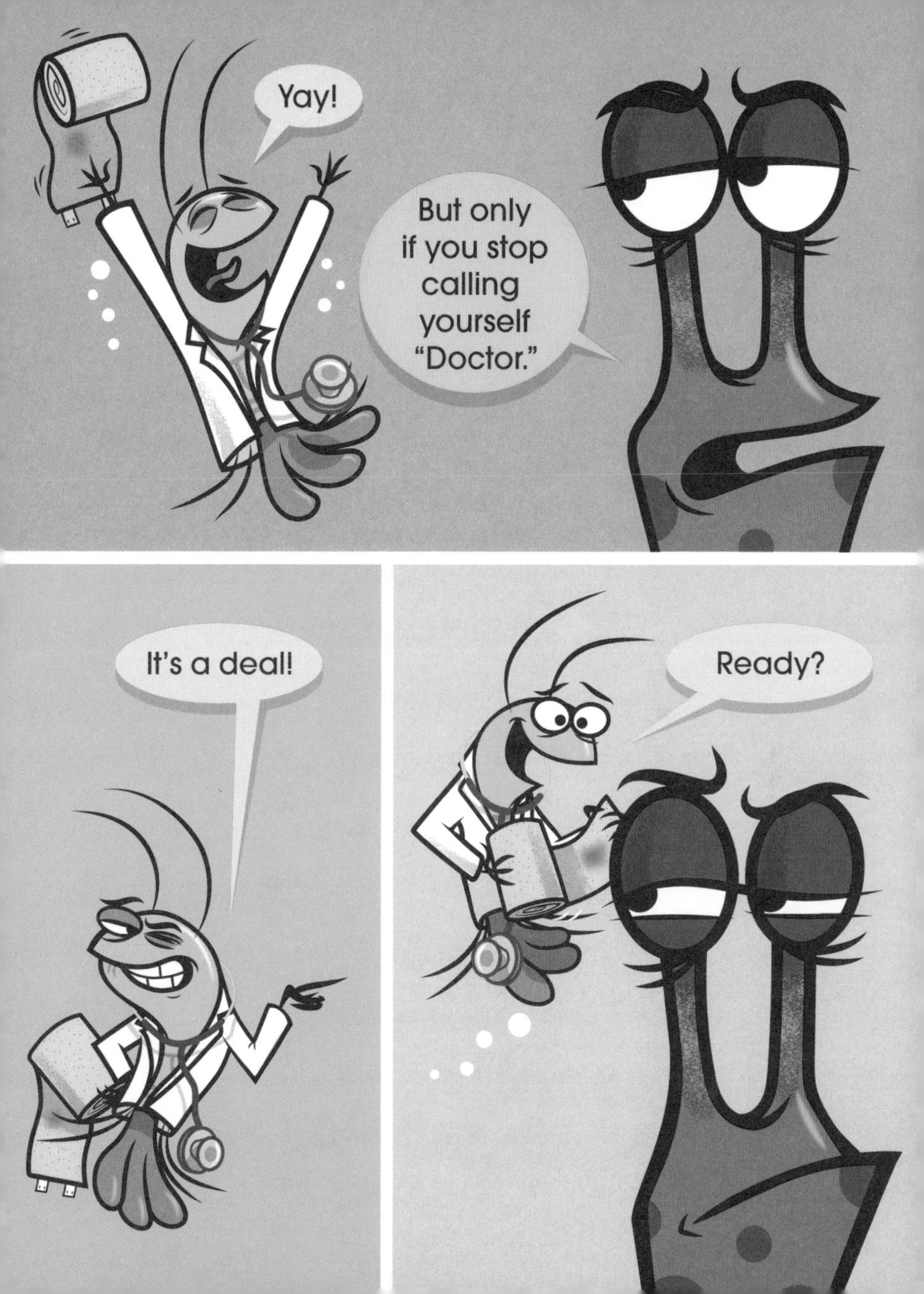
Yay!
But only if you stop calling yourself "Doctor."
It's a deal!
Ready?

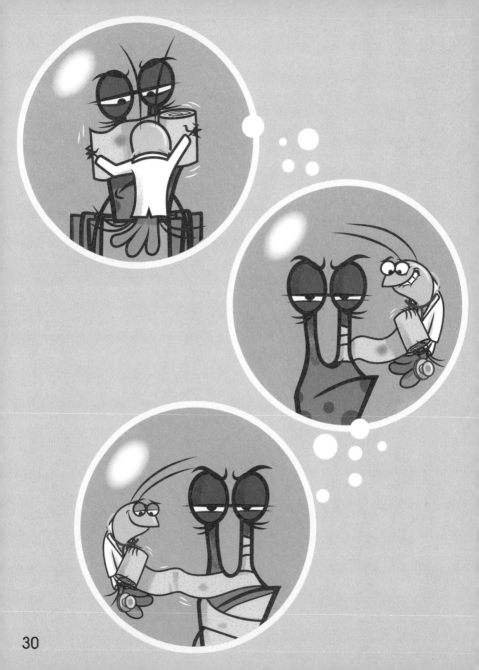

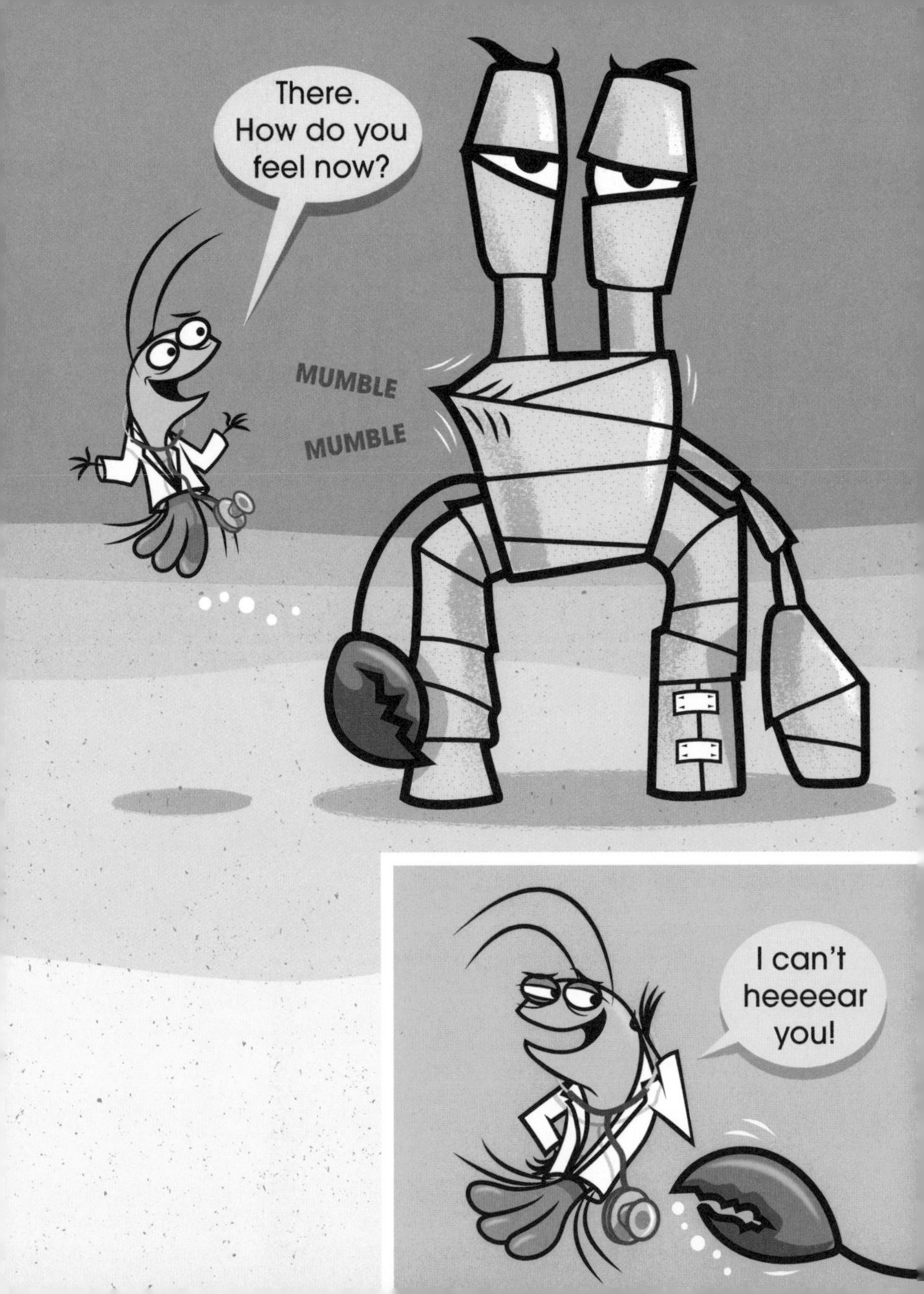

There. How do you feel now?
MUMBLE
MUMBLE
I can't heeeear you!

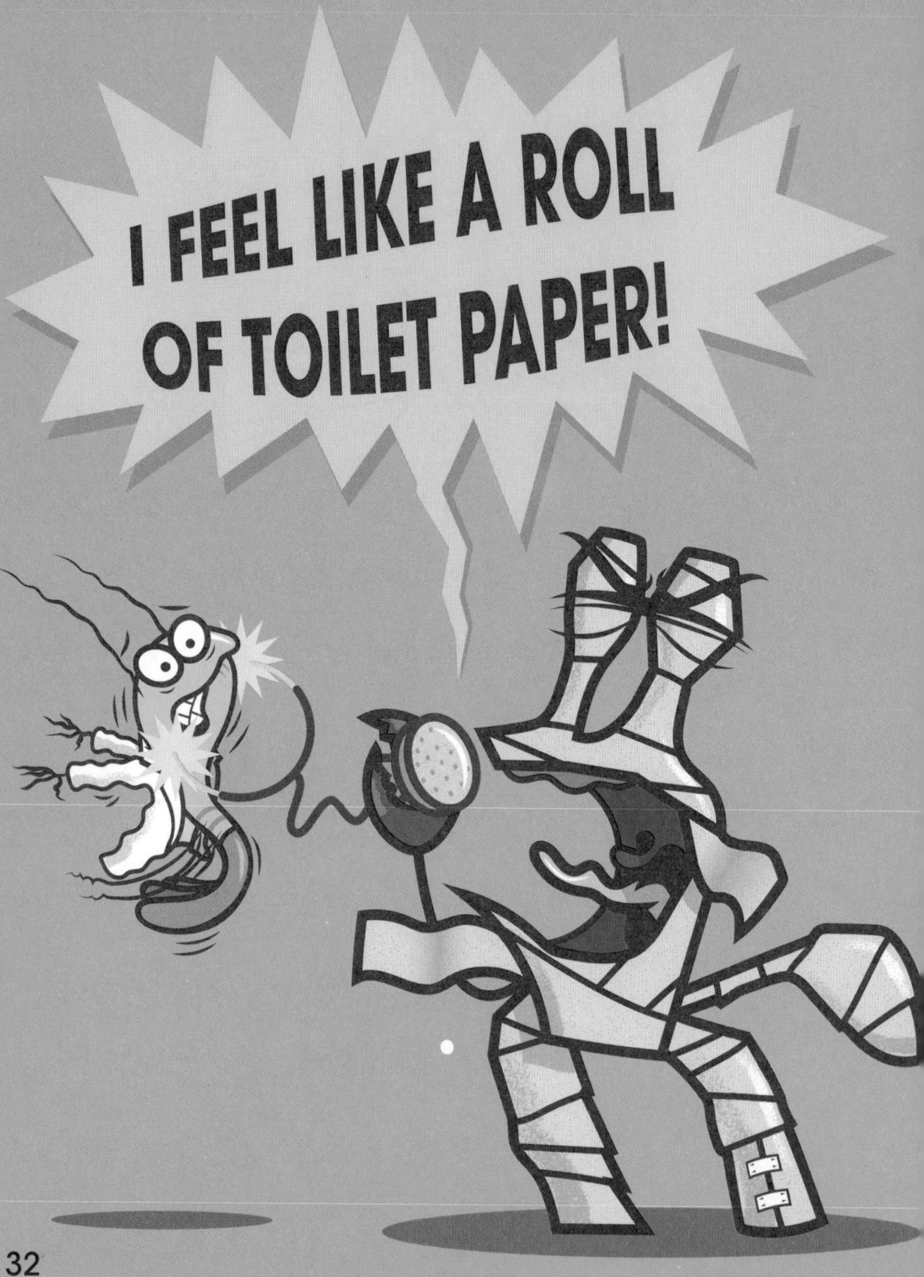
I FEEL LIKE A ROLL OF TOILET PAPER!

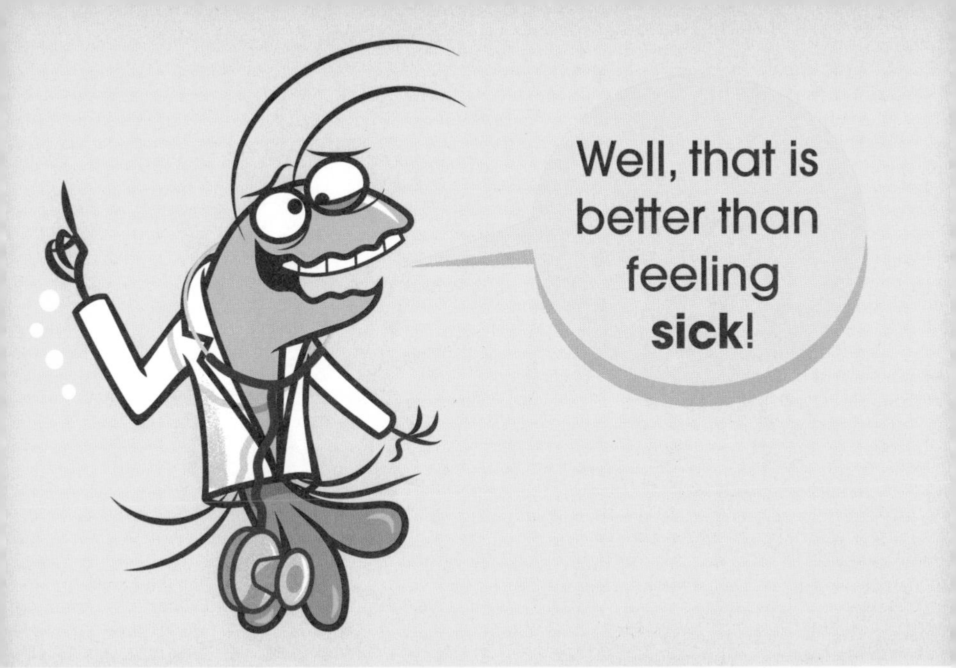
Well, that is better than feeling **sick**!

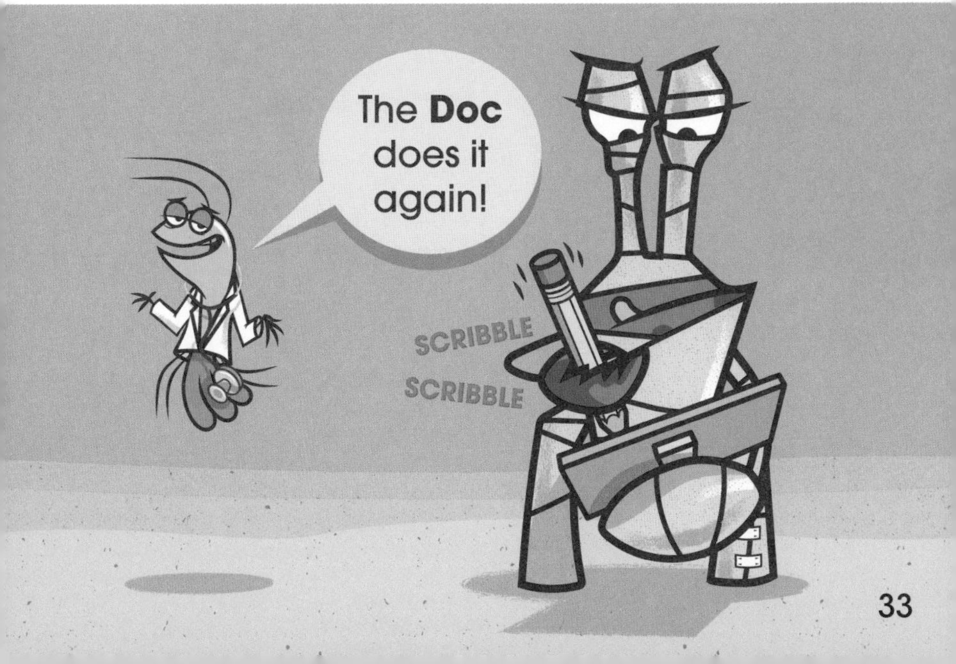
The **Doc** does it again!
SCRIBBLE
SCRIBBLE

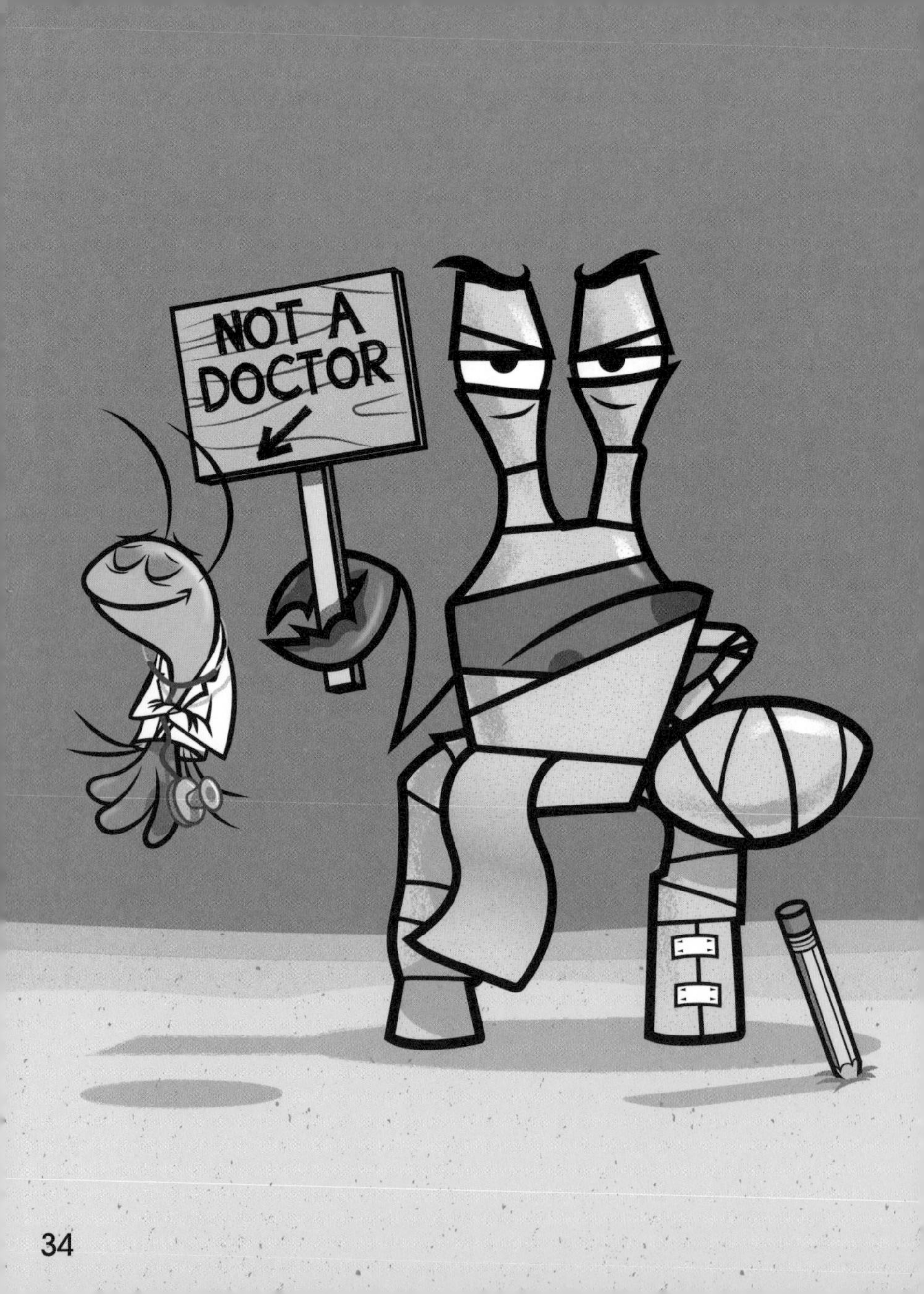
NOT A
DOCTOR

THE CURE

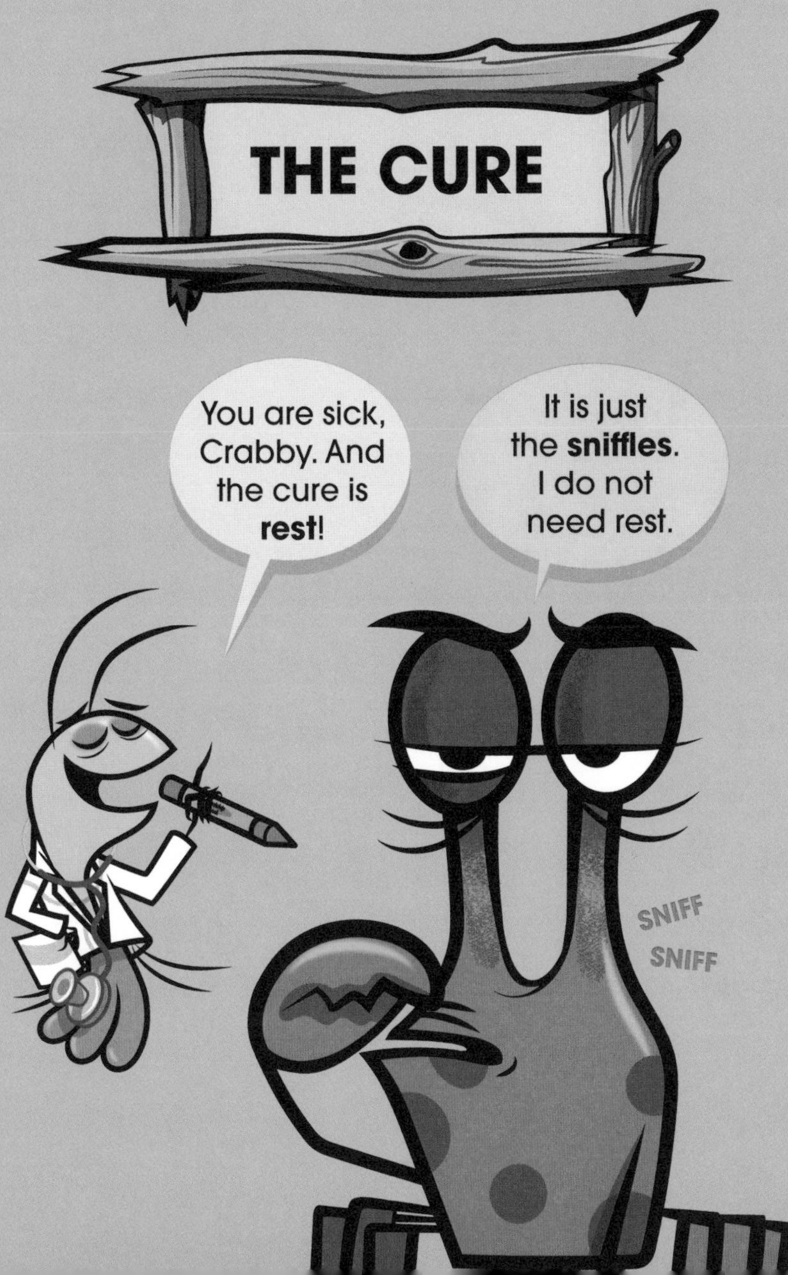
You are sick, Crabby. And the cure is **rest**!
It is just the **sniffles**. I do not need rest.
SNIFF
SNIFF

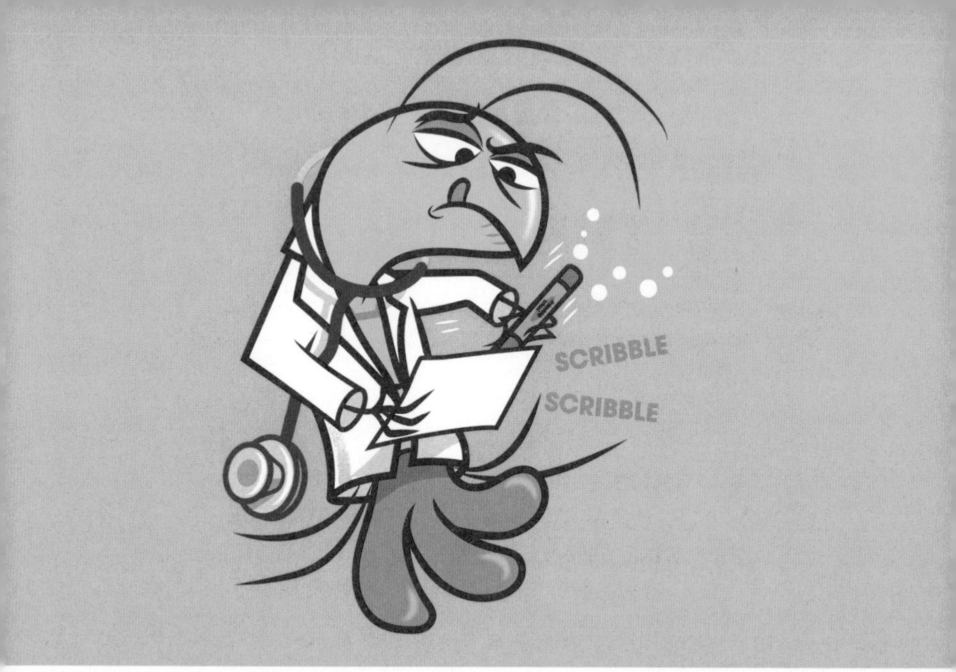
SCRIBBLE
SCRIBBLE

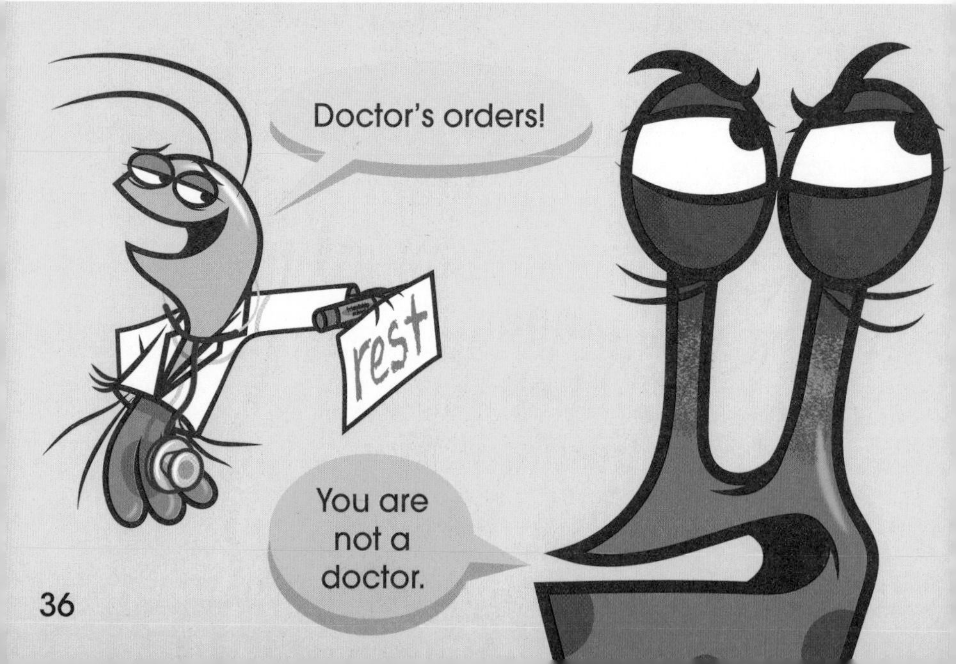
Doctor's orders!
rest
You are not a doctor.

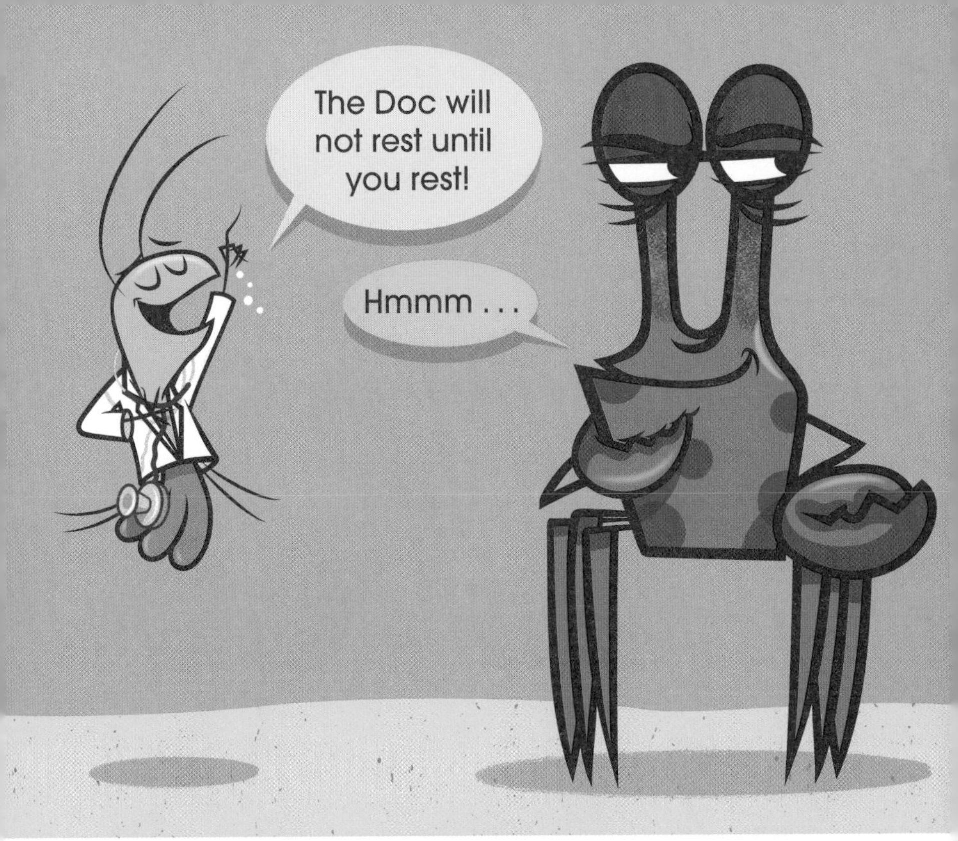
The Doc will not rest until you rest!
Hmmm . . .

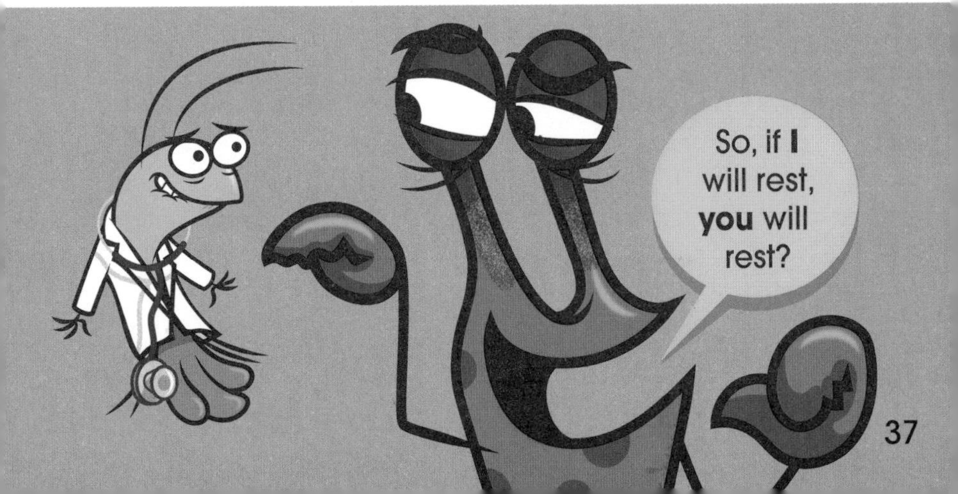
So, if **I** will rest, **you** will rest?

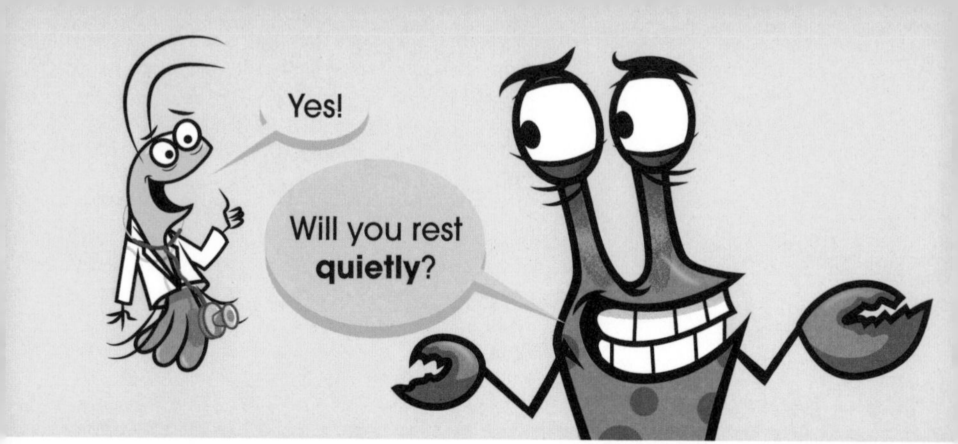
Yes!
Will you rest **quietly**?

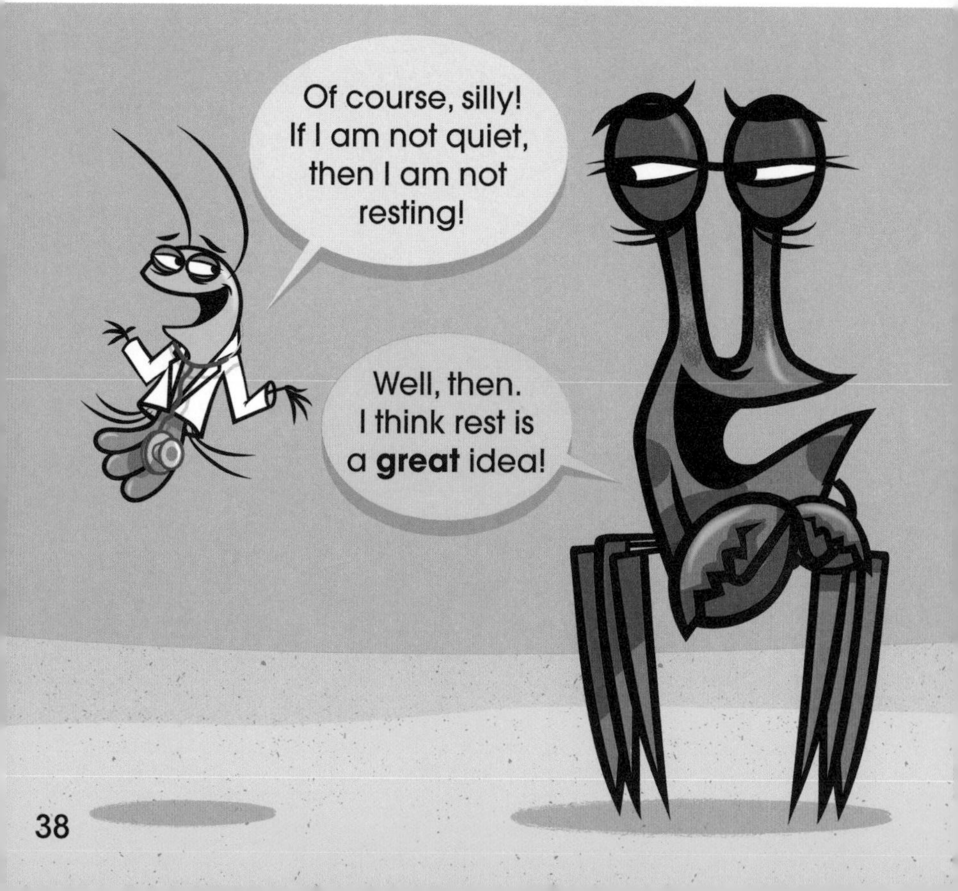
Of course, silly! If I am not quiet, then I am not resting!
Well, then. I think rest is a **great** idea!

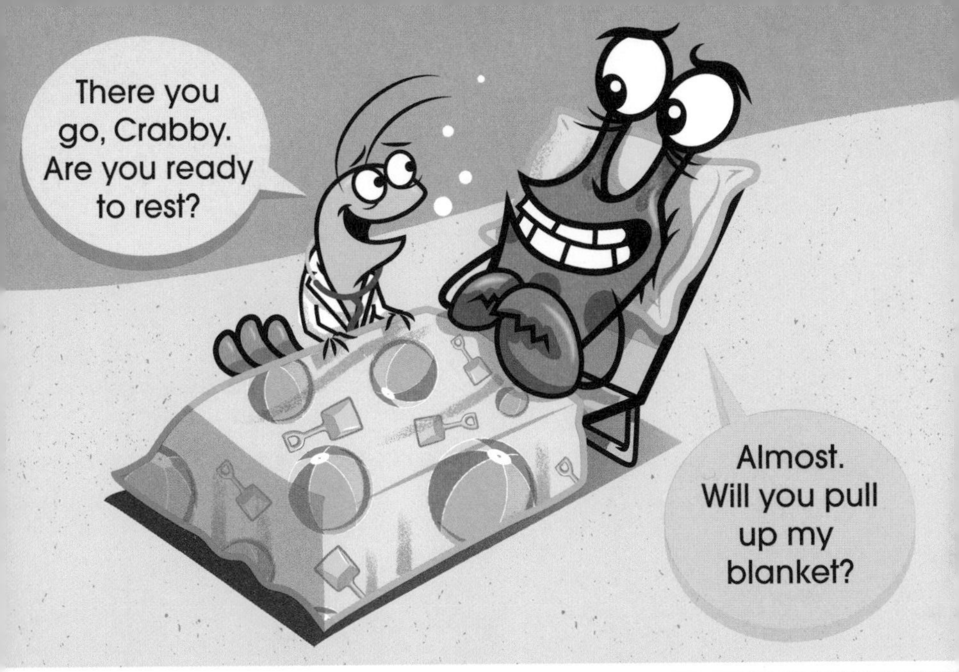
There you go, Crabby. Are you ready to rest?
Almost. Will you pull up my blanket?

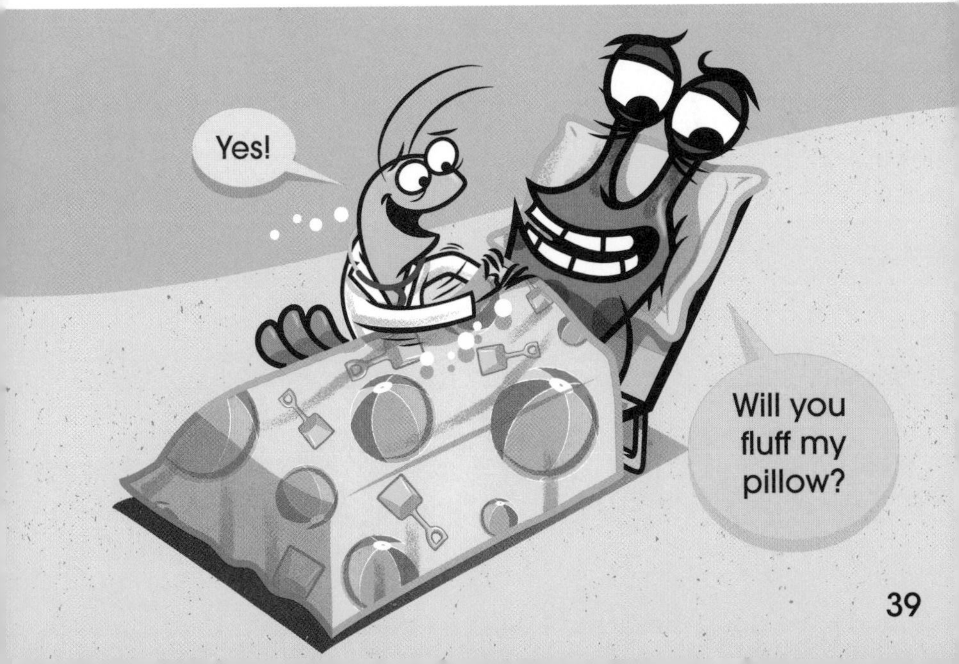
Yes!
Will you fluff my pillow?

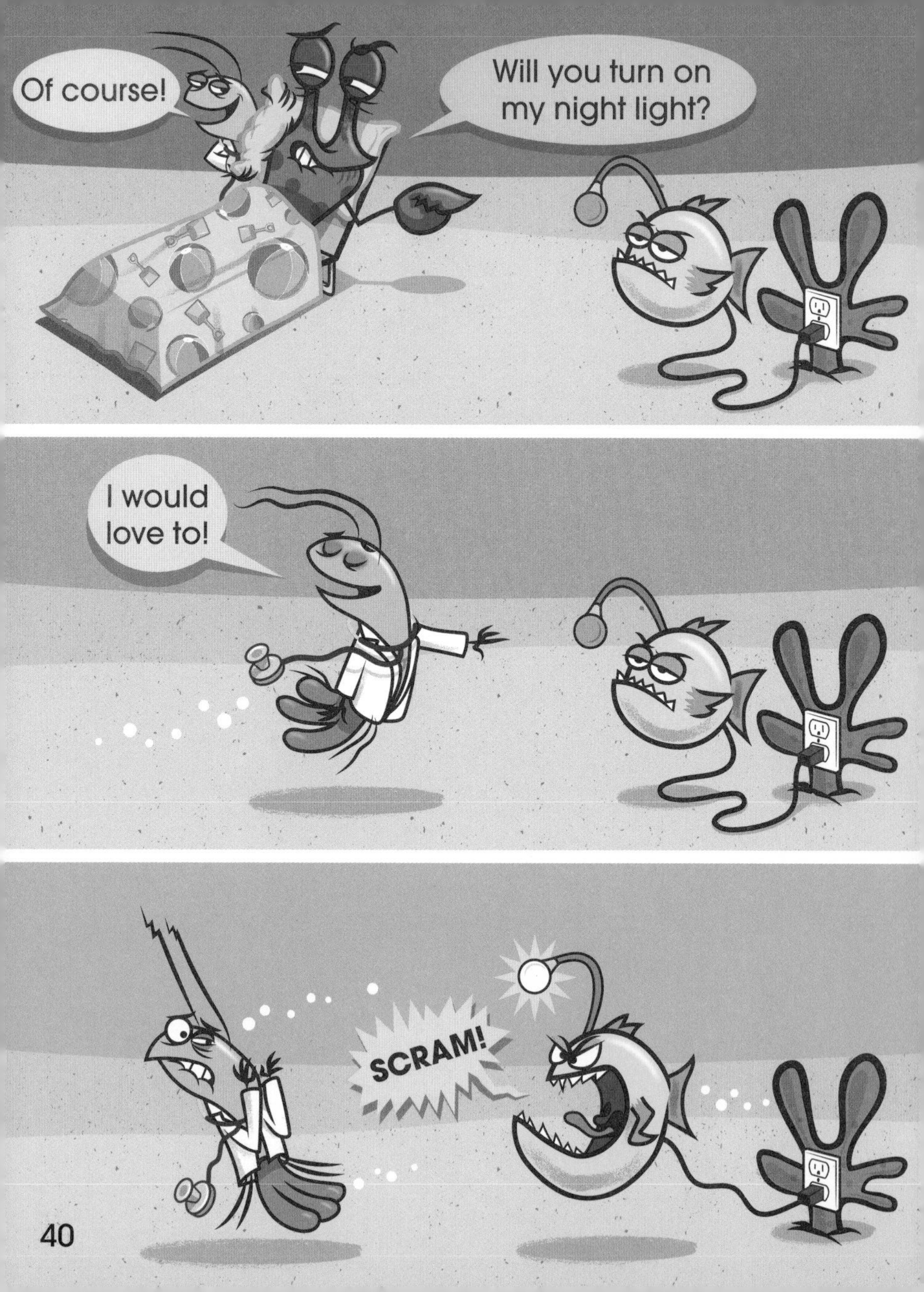
Will you turn on my night light?
Of course!
I would love to!
SCRAM!

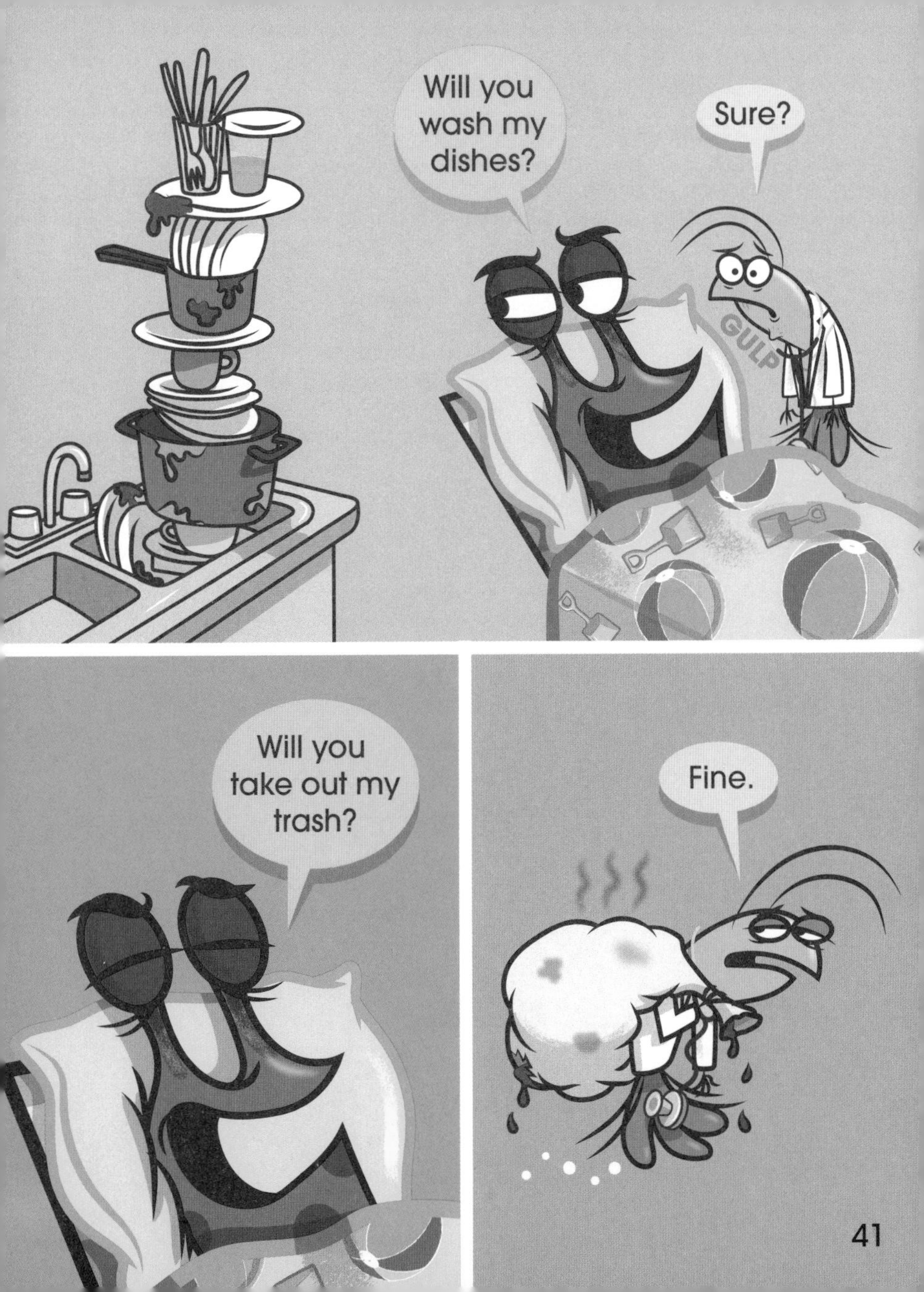
Will you wash my dishes?
Sure?
GULP
Will you take out my trash?
Fine.

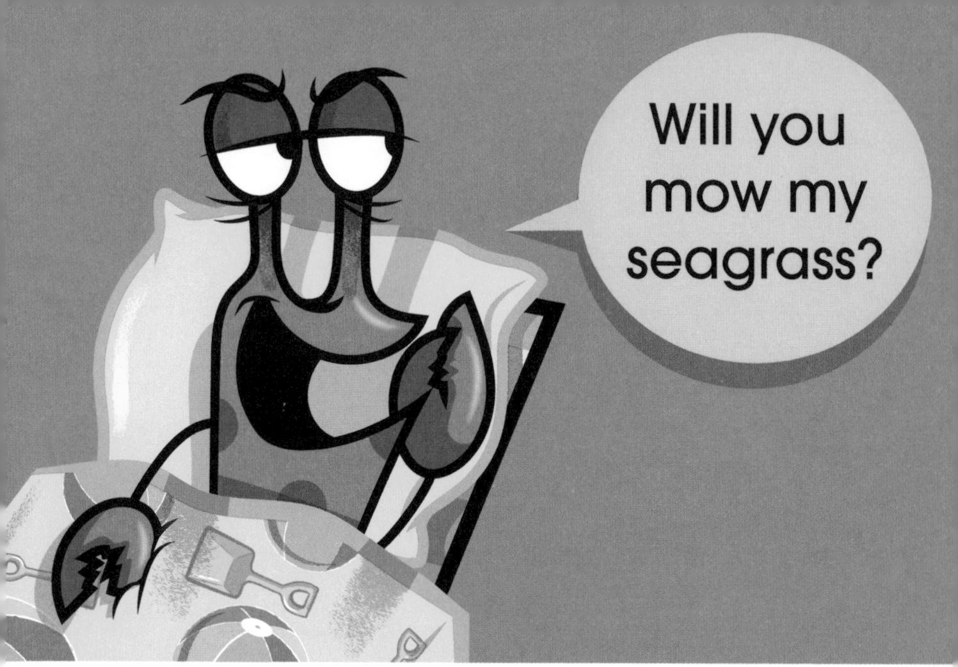
Will you mow my seagrass?

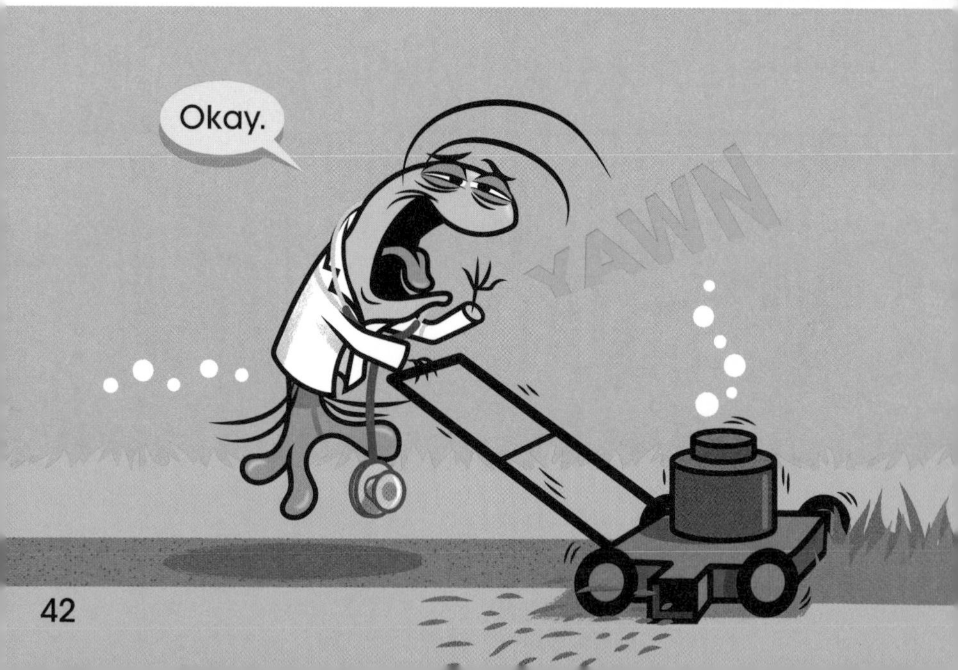
Okay.
YAWN

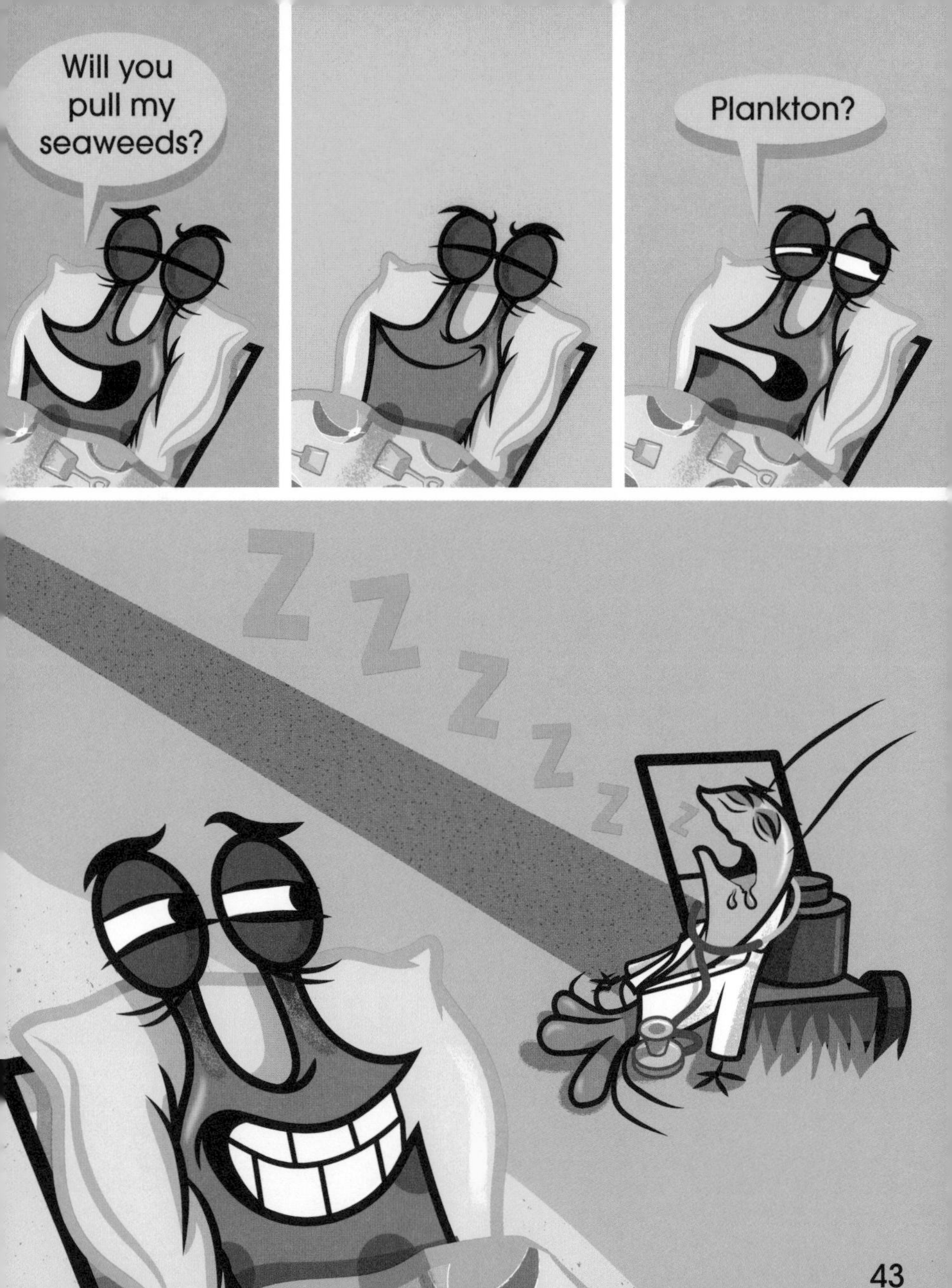
Will you pull my seaweeds?
Plankton?
Z Z Z Z Z Z

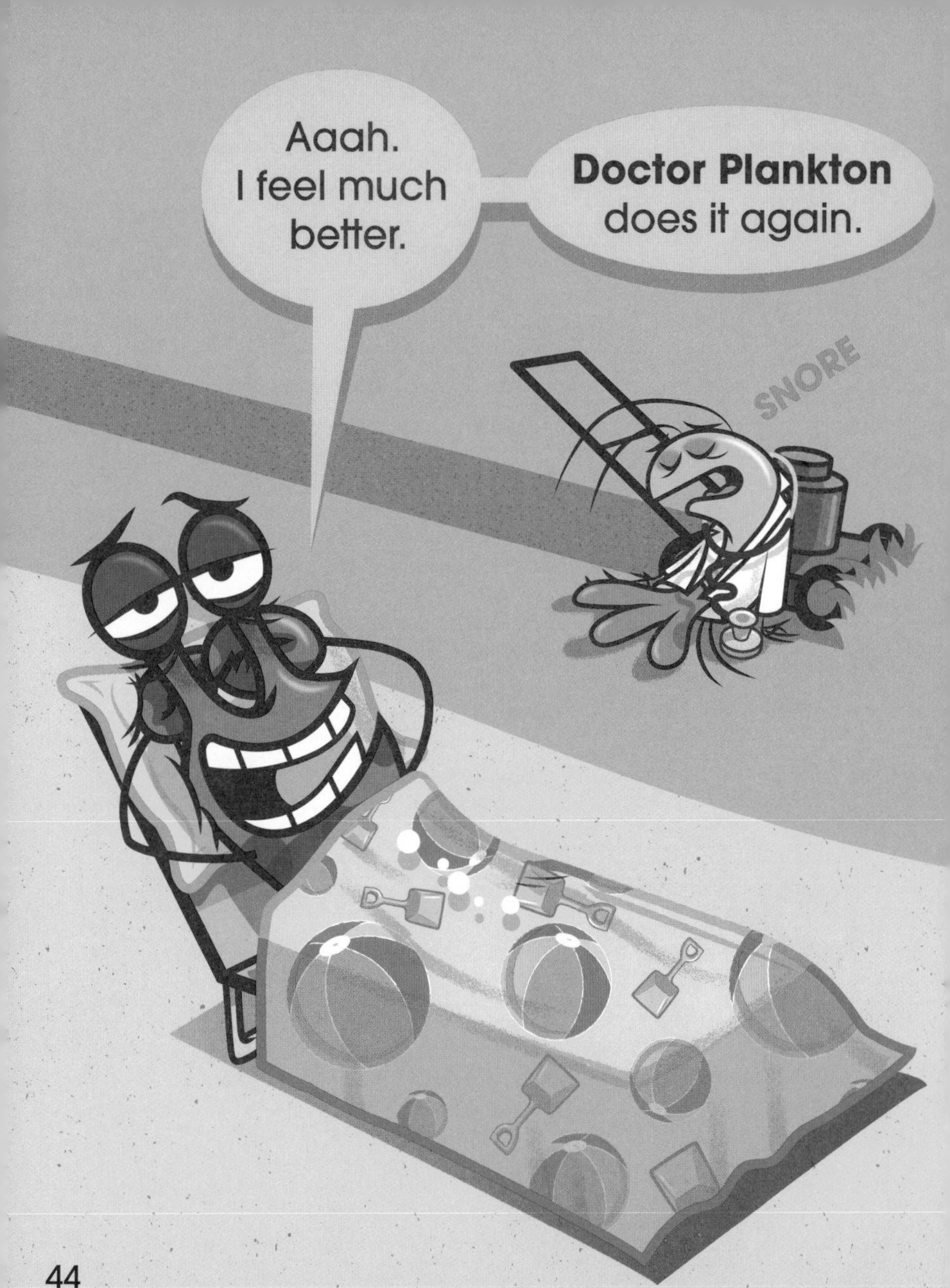

Aaah. I feel much better.
Doctor Plankton does it again.
SNORE

About the Author

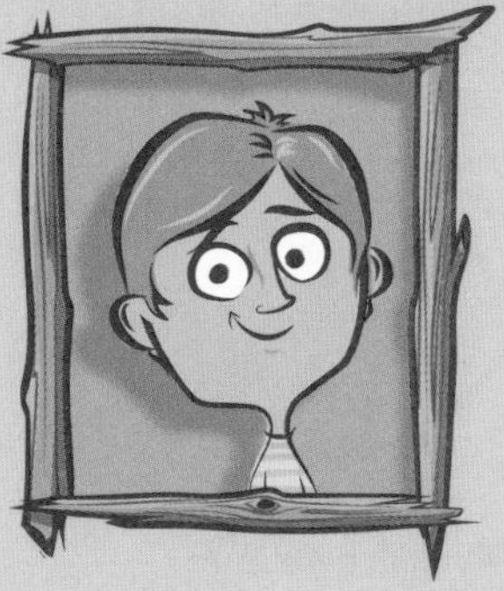

Jonathan Fenske lives in South Carolina with his family. He was born in Florida near the ocean, so he knows all about life at the beach! He thinks the worst part about being sick is having to miss playtime!

Jonathan is the author and illustrator of several children's books including **Barnacle Is Bored**, **Plankton Is Pushy** (a Junior Library Guild selection), and **After Squidnight** (an Indie Next Pick). His early reader **A Pig, a Fox, and a Box** was a Theodor Seuss Geisel Honor Book.

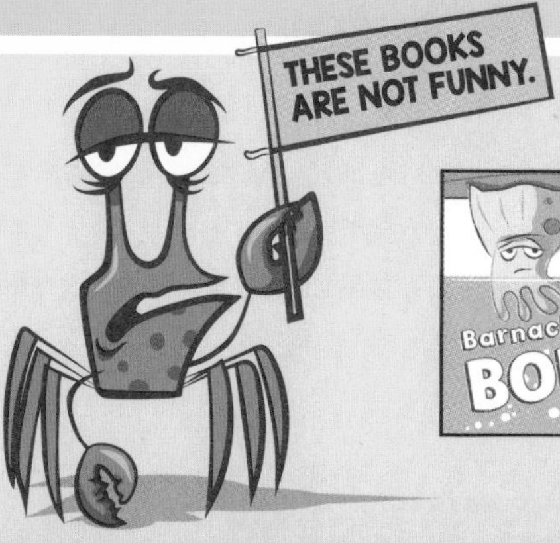
THESE BOOKS ARE NOT FUNNY.

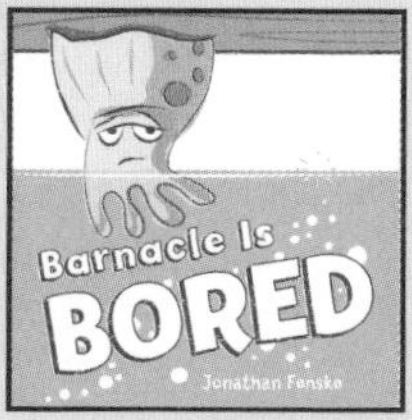
Barnacle Is
BORED
Jonathan Fenske

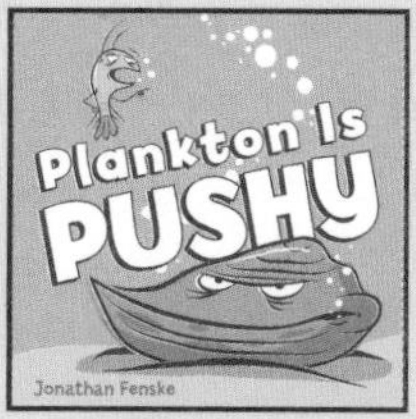
Plankton Is
PUSHY
Jonathan Fenske

YOU CAN DRAW CLAMMY!

I'm as happy as a clam!

1. Draw a football shape.

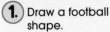

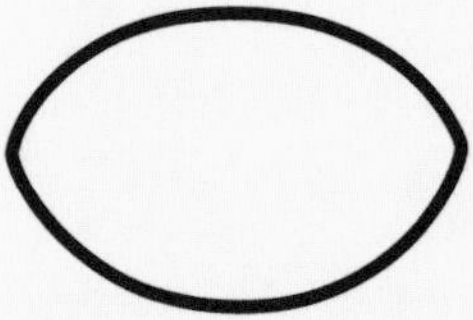

2. Make one long squiggly line and one small curved line for the mouth.

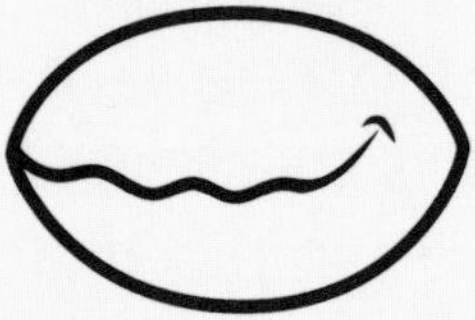

3. Add two circles for eyes.

4. Give Clammy an expression by adding lines and dots to the eyes.

5. Color Clammy with your favorite colors!

6. Add some fun details for decoration!

WHAT'S YOUR STORY?

Crabby is sick! Plankton tries to help Crabby feel better.
How would **you** try to help Crabby feel better?
Would Plankton and Clammy help you take care of Crabby?
Write and draw your story!

scholastic.com/acorn